Scandalous SCOT

SCANDALOUS SCOT

CECELIA MECCA

ALTIORA PRESS

Thank you to my sister who continues to be one of my biggest supporters. Love you Jena.

NEW ORLEANS, **Louisiana**
Present Day

AND JUST LIKE THAT, Reik was gone too, leaving Ian alone in the cavernous house.

How many times had Ian looked around the Quarter and said to himself, *I've seen stranger shit than that?* Having grown up in a place with a history of accepting the unwanted, the "freaks" of society . . . Ian was pretty much used to anything.

But this took the cake.

All three of his damn brothers had officially disappeared, presumably into the past.

Ian stared at the ancient silver cross in his hands, the one he and his brother had been holding together a few minutes earlier. It was unnaturally cold, but it hardly looked like a relic that had the power to send one person into the past, let alone three. And yet, there was no denying Rhys, Grey, and Reikart had all disappeared while holding it.

This was some crazy shit. But he couldn't sit here all day and dwell on it. He had work to do.

Laying the cross on his father's desk, he strode to the picture window, grateful it overlooked the private garden. St. Charles Ave. was probably swarmed with reporters curious about the increasingly strange affairs of the McCaim family. Dad in a coma. His brothers' disappearances getting more and more difficult to hide.

And wouldn't they have a field day with this?

Ian slipped his phone out of his perfectly tailored pants, which would only garner strange looks where he was going. He found his cousin's number, then called him on speaker and tossed the phone onto the mahogany desk next to him. It would only make him more anxious if he had to watch it shake in his hands.

"Reik's gone," he said as soon as his cousin answered.

Silence.

Jeremy, completely up to speed on everything that had happened since the day Rhys disappeared, must be beyond shock at this point.

"Jeremy?"

"I'm here. It's just . . ."

Yeah, I know.

The whole thing was nuts, which was why they'd assumed their father was crazy the moment the words *time travel* left his lips. For five years, he'd been claiming their mother hadn't left them—that she was, in fact, a time traveler from ancient Scotland who'd been called back to her time. The best investigators money could buy had disagreed, saying she'd walked away from the family and scrubbed her identity to avoid being found.

She didn't leave us. Your mom is from the past. I know it sounds crazy, but I'm going to prove it to you. When I figure out the chant, I will prove it.

They hadn't laughed him off—he was their dad, after all—

but they hadn't believed him either. Ian felt guilty for that now. They all did. Especially since their father was in a coma. His dedication to finding their mother had taken a toll on him, and he'd suffered a breakdown.

"We worked it out. Jeremy . . ." Ian closed his eyes, blocking out the bright sun streaming in through the picture windows. "I'm going too. You know what to do."

More silence.

Jeremy would serve as McCaim Shipping's interim director and take the lead in convening executive sessions. If they weren't back in two weeks, he would step in to help lead Ian's public relations team, the one he'd put together over the last four years. After a month, a search firm would be hired to replace all four of the brothers.

They'd come close to losing the business when his mom had first gone missing. Investors had lost faith in the McCaim patriarch, and they'd threatened to walk—so Rhys and Grey had done the hard thing and forced their father out. But Rhys and Grey were gone, and Reik and Ian had agreed they would stop at nothing to go with them. While Ian had wanted to try again immediately, Reik's cooler head had prevailed. He'd reminded Ian that they were the only two McCaim brothers left in good enough health to run the company. Provisions had to be made. For the company. For their father.

Mom had been gone for five years. What if they were gone as long?

What if they never came back at all? Without the cross, they couldn't get back. Presumably. And it was still here in his father's study.

So they'd made their contingency plan. Told their cousin everything to ensure someone would be here for Dad, someone with the best interests of McCaim Shipping in mind.

Now it was time to put it into action.

"Jesus, Ian. I can't believe this. I mean, I *do* believe you, but . . . he's seriously gone?"

Ian turned to look at the spot Reik had occupied moments before.

"He's gone. And I can't screw around here. None of us knows how the rules work. If I don't do this right now, who knows when, or where, I'll end up. This way, at least I'll have a good shot at finding Reik."

"Are you prepared?"

Ian moved toward the duffle bag he'd prepared.

"More than Rhys and Grey, for sure," he said, unzipping the bag. He hadn't even changed from work yet. But unlike when he and Reik grabbed the cross earlier, as they'd done most days since Rhys had vanished in front of them, this time, he knew it would work.

He'd watched first Rhys, then Grey, then Reik succeed where he'd failed . . . He knew now which word had tripped him up and was confident he would be joining his brothers next.

"And you're sure about this?"

Ian tried to ignore the censure in Jeremy's voice. His cousin didn't understand the choice he was facing: abandon his mother and brothers in the past or his father and the company he'd built in the present. In the end, nothing mattered more than his family, and the doctor had made it clear that his dad was all but screwed. His brain was still swollen, his prospects dim. So he would go back, find his brothers and mother, and use this silver cross to bring them all back.

Maybe, just maybe, hearing their mother's voice again would bring their father back too.

He had to hope.

"I'm sure." He began taking off his dress shoes. "Thank you, Jeremy."

"Good luck, cuz. I have a feeling you're going to need it."

Ian pulled off his socks next and then dumped the jeans, T-shirt, and hoodie out from his bag. What was one supposed to wear to time travel, anyway?

Certainly not a suit.

"Take care of him." Ian would not get emotional again. He and Reik had already visited the hospital to say their goodbyes to a father who couldn't hear them.

"Will do."

This time, the silence wasn't broken by his cousin's voice. Jeremy had hung up.

Ian finished changing, and before his brother could get too far ahead of him—if that was even how this worked—he grabbed the cross and took a deep breath.

He'd only been this scared three times in his life.

The night they'd learned their mother was missing. The day they'd gotten the call that their dad was in the hospital. And the first time one of his brothers had disappeared before their eyes. And now he was about to follow in his older brothers' footsteps, as he'd always done, for better or worse.

Ian's hands refused to stop shaking. What a chickenshit he was.

Just say the words.

He didn't need the slip of paper anymore, Ian knew them by heart. He'd listened to Reik's recording of the words over and over again. His brother hadn't thought he was listening—it wasn't something he was known for in the family—but this time, he had been all ears.

Roll the gh *on the last word.*

"*Talamh, èadhar, teine, usige ga thilleadh dhachaigh.*"

2

KINROSS CASTLE, **Scotland**
March 1286

"PLEASE? Just a wee moment alone with him? I will ask Cook to make burrebrede this eve."

Màiri had her maid now. Everyone knew how much Alana loved burrebrede. She had to relent. She simply had to. Ambrose was here in the castle, and Màiri had not seen him for more than a fortnight. If she did not speak with him privately now, she wasn't sure when she'd have a chance. She could ask her father for permission to walk to the loch, the only other way she'd have a chance to see him alone, but she doubted her father would agree to such a scheme given the snow.

Nay, Màiri was determined to see him now. Without a chaperone.

"If your father learns of it . . ."

Màiri leaned forward and kissed the maid on her wrinkled cheek.

Alana frowned. "As if I could not ask Muir to make burrebrede myself," she muttered.

Knowing it had been a weak plan all along, she wrinkled her nose. "You know I'd never do anything untoward."

Alana had a way of chastening Màiri with a mere gesture, and she did so now. A slight widening of her eyes reminded Màiri of *that* summer.

"'Twas one kiss. And I told you straightaway."

"One kiss"—Alana adjusted her cap—"with a man who will ne'er be yer husband."

The expression on her face stung more than the words. She clearly meant what she said. She did not believe Màiri's father would ever allow them to marry.

"Do not look at me so. You know it well, my lady. And you also know what your father would think if he were ever to find out."

Màiri refrained from chastising her for the formal address. She had spent as many years as she could speak asking Alana to use her given name. She was no maid. In all ways but one, this woman was her mother.

And yet, as in most things, Alana sided with Màiri's stubborn father. If he decided it was in their clan's best interest to build ships and sail his entire clan into the North Sea, Alana would think it the wisest plan any laird had ever devised.

"I know my father wishes it not to be so," Màiri said softly, looking away. "But perhaps he will change his mind."

She didn't need Alana's look of skepticism to know her words rang hollow.

"Go. Be quick about it before your father learns of his presence. He shouldn't be here."

Màiri didn't need to be told twice. She ran from her bedchamber through the halls of the castle where she'd been raised. Although she hadn't asked Alana, she knew where Ambrose would be: the solar belowstairs. It had been her mother's preferred place, and her father still avoided it so many years after her death.

Slowing her pace before approaching the open door, she took a moment to compose herself and then stepped inside.

With the winter winds howling outside, the largest window in the entire castle providing evidence that it was, indeed, snowing again, the fire Ambrose stood in front of roared. He was looking at the carved overmantel, the story of Adam and Eve etched into its stone.

"Ambrose?"

He turned, the familiar face of her childhood friend softening as he looked from her to the open door behind her.

"Alana?"

"Has agreed to give us a moment alone."

Long dark-blond hair capped a slightly long but nevertheless handsome face. Once their friendship had been sanctioned by their fathers. But that had been many years ago, before the men had taken different sides in a fight Màiri wished to forget.

"My apologies for not coming sooner. My father . . ."

His voice trailed off as it always did when he spoke of Laird Dern.

"I'm pleased you came today," she said honestly. With so few age-mates at Kinross, she'd always sought out Ambrose for company and conversation. He was also the one person who never, ever, stared at her cheek. It was as if he didn't notice her mark at all.

She gestured to the bench on the other side of the sole wooden table in the room. He sat, and Màiri did the same. On the other side, of course. Though her father was still likely in the hall, where he spent much of his time during the day, it would not do well for them to sit on the same bench together.

Father Abernethy would have much to say about such an arrangement, particularly without a chaperone present.

"I spoke to my father about us," Ambrose said.

The thudding in her chest had nothing to do with any uncertainty about taking Ambrose as her husband. She wanted that. More than anything. Had wanted it for nigh on a year now, ever since he first suggested it.

They were a perfect match.

He had an easy temperament, much like hers, and their friendship had endured the breakup of their clans' alliance. She and Ambrose had just one hurdle: their fathers despised each other.

"What did he say?"

Ambrose tried to smile. "He did not toss me from the room."

"As I should do now?" a deep voice asked.

Màiri sighed, not even attempting to disguise the sound. Of course her father would have discovered Ambrose was here. The man knew everything. How had she thought it might be possible for them to steal a few moments alone? Slowly, she turned toward the door. Ambrose was already standing as if her father were his commander in battle.

"Ambrose has done nothing wrong."

The argument sounded tired, even to her own ears.

Her father didn't move. Filling the doorway with his frame, he stood immobile, attempting to intimidate poor Ambrose. Fortunately, her friend knew him well and did not react.

"Where is Alana?" Her father did not sound pleased.

She was tempted to ask if his curiosity had more to do with her and Ambrose being alone together, or if he wished to know for his own purposes. Màiri had long suspected their feelings for each other extended past the typical relationship between a master and servant, but all of her attempts to unite them had come to naught.

"I came straight to the solar when I heard Ambrose had arrived," she lied. Although Alana could handle her father easily enough without help, she had no wish to be at the center of an argument between them. "Father, please. Ambrose was just . . ."

She wasn't certain about how to finish.

"Leaving." Her father was never at a loss for words.

"Aye," Ambrose agreed, walking toward the door. "I was leaving."

She pleaded with her eyes for him to stand up to her father, to refuse to leave until they finished their conversation. But Ambrose would never do that. He claimed disagreeing with her father was no way to win his respect.

When her father stood aside, Ambrose nodded his fare-thee-well, clearly uncomfortable with having to navigate the burly laird.

Màiri had no such qualms.

"You could have allowed him to stay," she snapped. "He just arrived."

Her father cared as much for Ambrose's feelings as he did for troubadours. Or his neighbors.

Very little.

"Ah, mhuirnín . . ."

"No. I am not your darling, not at this moment."

She loved her father dearly. Understood his hurt, his anger. But that did not mean she was prepared to forgive him for refusing to consider her feelings.

"Pardon me, Father."

Attempting to ignore the look of hurt on his face, Màiri pushed past him to retreat to her chamber. Another afternoon of crocheting, one that could have been spent in pleasant conversation with the man she loved.

And if it was not the type of love troubadours sang of, so be it. She was determined Ambrose would become her husband one day, with or without her father's approval.

3

Ian had been right to be terrified.

Hurtling through time felt sort of like waking up with a raging hangover and finding yourself on a Tilt-a-Whirl all at once. At least he'd been prepared for it. How the hell had Rhys, or his mother for that matter, managed? Even though he'd expected it to be uncomfortable, the force of it made the shuttle launch experience at Kennedy Space Center feel like a horse and buggy ride.

Finally, it stopped. Ian was afraid to open his eyes at first, but as soon as his stomach settled, he immediately began to shiver. A natural consequence of sitting in knee-deep snow. He opened his eyes, and pretty much all he could see was snow and trees. Maybe if he stood . . .

Yeah, not going to happen.

Ian breathed in and out for a good five minutes, his body somewhere between fight and flight. He tried again. This time, his legs supported him. Kind of. He felt like a baby foal, or at least what he imagined one would feel like.

Holy shit.

What he hadn't been able to see from the ground was a castle looming on a distant hill like a huge beacon. Three towers encased in never-ending walls, surrounded by nothing but snow-covered trees and a muddy path not far from him that was also more snow-covered than cleared.

He moved closer to the path. It lacked any car tracks or wheel imprints, but there were plenty of hoofprints.

He stepped onto the path, snow seeping into his sneakers, the cross still thankfully clutched in his hand, and tried to calm the fuck down. His hands shook, more than they had in his father's study, the castle in front of him going in and out of focus.

It wasn't possible. And yet, here he was. But where was here exactly? This had to be Scotland, right?

Where was Reik?

Only one way to get some answers.

One foot in front of the other. Like the time he'd played in a championship game with a broken ankle, throwing as many touchdowns as he had in his entire college football career. *Pretend everything is fine. Keep moving. It doesn't hurt. You didn't just travel through time.*

Except he did.

The evidence was right in front of him.

Reik's words ran through his head: *Her dad is Laird MacKinnish. Her brothers are Alastair, Ross, Dermot, and Colban. And a sister, Grace. Hopefully someone will know them and we can find our way to Hightower Castle if we don't start there.*

As Ian approached the castle, he caught sight of a few specks on the walls between the towers. Those were no tourists. He couldn't see what they wore or what kind of weapons they carried, but he'd seen enough movies to know they were guards.

Surrounded by cliffs on three sides, the castle rose high above him as he continued up the path. On the fourth side, a river flowed freely. His family had been to Scotland just once, but Ian was sure they had never come here. He would have remembered this place.

It was stunning.

And more than a bit scary. Did he just walk up in his jeans and Saints sweatshirt, cross in hand, declare himself Ian MacKinnish, and ask to see the person in charge?

He and Reik had talked about this, what would happen if they were successful. But nothing could have prepared him for the reality of it. Nor was any foolproof plan occurring to him now, as he approached the gatehouse. At least the path was smoother closer to the castle. His sneakers were covered in mud.

He'd been spotted.

Ian still couldn't see any of the guards clearly, but there was suddenly a frenzy of activity up there, and a man appeared above him. Still woozy, his quads burning from the effort of the climb, Ian looked up to the guard, a long-ass sword hanging at his side.

What should he say? *Hello? How's it going?* What would sound less conspicuous?

"Whit ye called?"

Ian could barely understand the man, but he knew one thing for sure. He was definitely in Scotland.

"I'm lost," he tried, aware he must look a fright to them. By now, the guard was surrounded by some of his closest and fiercest-looking friends.

Another flurry of activity.

Ian stared at the crisscross of iron bars in front of him with a passageway leading into the castle. A portcullis, if he remembered correctly from the tours. He couldn't see much on the other side through the bars, but when he looked up, the men were gone. Literally gone.

By now his body had returned somewhat to normal.

He wasn't one to panic, but suddenly all of the possibilities that had swirled in his head since Rhys disappeared crystallized. How likely was it any of them had survived? He only hoped his brothers had faced death more honorably than he was sure to.

Because Ian was fucking terrified.

Cold, groggy, but fully aware of his tenuous position, Ian watched as the portcullis was finally lifted on the other end of the tunnel in front of him. Two men ducked under it and came toward him.

Ian's heart slammed in his chest.

No.

It couldn't be.

4

"GOOD DAY, LADY MÀIRI."

It was a fine day indeed. Or would be soon.

"Good day, Boyd. Will you saddle Gil for me?"

He looked at her precisely as he should have given she was demanding such a thing when she appeared to be without an escort. But Màiri's tone did not allow for questioning. She'd learned some things, after all, as the daughter of Alexander Kelbrue, laird of Clan Kelbrue, a man feared by all—including her, at times. But most of the time he was simply her father, and an indulgent one at that. He'd allowed her to refuse a proposal from the son of the laird of Clan Tavish, a match he'd quite liked, and when she'd asked to accompany her father to the Tournament of the North, he'd agreed despite the risks of traveling along the border.

For nigh on twenty-two years, he'd given her everything, and more.

But not this time. He refused to budge when it came to Ambrose's suit.

"Are ye ready, my lady?" Boyd asked, his expression still doubious.

She was indeed. The snow had prevented her from riding this last sennight, and she was desperate to leave the castle. None gave her notice as she rode across the bridge and over the frozen moat below. Father would be wroth when he learned she'd gone alone, but Màiri knew this path better than most. Besides, the rebuilding of the sluice that had caused the moat to freeze had him more occupied than usual. It was possible he'd not learn of her ride at all.

But not likely.

Gil moved slowly in the snow, but her trustworthy steed knew the way. Reaching a gloved hand to her hood, Màiri tugged the fur closer around her cheeks. She despised the cold, but being trapped inside was an even worse fate.

According to Father, her mother had felt the same way. Being out of doors had filled her with happiness, the kind of happiness that, despite their arranged marriage, had made him fall in love. He'd told Màiri quite a bit about her mother, but the stories lacked the depth of actual memories. If only she could remember her mother's smile, her voice.

"Good boy," she said as Gil navigated his way toward the loch.

Since she did not expect to see anyone, not at this time of year, a movement instantly caught her eye. The loch Clan Kelbrue shared with their now enemies, Clan Dern, had for years stood between them. Now it served as a reminder of broken promises and shifting allegiances. Even so, she continued to favor the spot, which was even more beautiful wreathed with the freshly fallen snow. All the better that she sometimes saw Ambrose here.

The movement she'd noticed became more prominent. Oddly, it seemed to be coming from the west, where their land bordered Clan MacKinnish. Few visitors or travelers had come from that direction since her father had broken his short-lived alliance with Robert the Bruce, whom the MacKinnishes still faithfully served. Periodically a MacKinnish might attempt to sway her father, but that had happened less frequently over the past months.

None of the visitors had been dangerous, but Màiri nevertheless retrieved her knife from her saddlebag. Slipping the weapon into the folds of her mantle, Màiri continued riding toward the loch, grateful the sun had decided to accompany her this day. She filled her chest with the crisp air, cold but not unbearable.

When she arrived at the lakeside, Màiri tied Gil to a tree and took out the bit of bread Muir had forced on her this morn. Then she strained her neck to see over the ridge where she thought she'd seen a rider.

There!

He, or she, was alone. Like her. And definitely approaching from the west. How very strange. The MacKinnishes rarely rode this far onto their property, which suggested this visitor intended to make yet another attempt to sway her father.

But it would not help.

He was now as set against the Bruce as he'd once been supportive of him. If there was one thing her father hated, it was a man who acted alone. And Bruce had done just that when he'd attacked John Balliol, another potential heir to the throne, after the envoy for the Guardians of Scotland was sent to the English court. He'd made the attack without consulting any of his allies.

The final mark, her father had said.

And now Clan Kelbrue stood against Bruce. To some, they were traitors because of it.

So be it.

Popping the last bite of bread into her mouth, Màiri decided not to wait for the rider to approach. Her father's warnings rang in her ears, and as much as she despised the idea of returning to the castle so soon, she turned around to do just that. Or at least she attempted it. She stumbled on an exposed root.

Her ankle.

Reaching down, she cursed it as she'd done so many times before. But it had been years since the injury troubled her. Like when she was younger, the jostling made it throb with pain, reminding Màiri of a day she dearly wished to forget.

The day she'd come back from that riding lesson to learn her mother had died.

WAS IT A WOMAN?

Ian couldn't tell from this distance. But one thing was for sure: he was definitely lost and should probably go back to look for his brother.

Who would have thought Greyson would be one of the first people he'd meet in medieval Scotland?

Ian shook his head, still incredulous at his good luck. The castle he'd approached, swarming with armed guards, had proven to be none other than Hightower, his mother's ancestral home, and the man who'd greeted him at the gates was his brother, albeit not the one he'd expected to find first.

"Ian!" Grey had screamed a week earlier, running toward him.

He'd stood frozen in place, unable to move, and only when his brother engulfed him in an uncharacteristic hug did the moment become real.

It was actually him.

Ian held on tight, probably for too long, judging by the slightly disgusted expression on his brother's hulking companion.

Turning toward the man, Grey grinned and said, "Meet Uncle Ross."

About a million questions had flocked Ian's head, but Grey had whispered for him to say nothing as he swept him through a wide open courtyard and yet another gatehouse. They entered the *keep*, as Grey called it, and poor Uncle Ross was left behind to answer questions about the jeans-wearing stranger while the two brothers headed up to Grey's bedchamber. By the time Ian had changed into some *more appropriate clothes* and began to warm up by the massive fireplace in his brother's room, he knew only three things:

Ian had found his way to Castle Hightower, their mother's ancestral home.

Mom and Rhys were here, in this time, but they were not at Hightower. And though Grey had reunited with their mother, he hadn't actually seen Rhys yet. It was a whole lot harder to get in touch with people in a time without cell phones or transport options other than horseback.

Reik was here too, but he'd apparently been here for months.

The answers he'd been given had only led to more questions.

He'd said as much, and Grey had just grinned. "I still can't believe you're here. And thank God you have the cross."

That was when the unreality of the situation had hit him again, hard. He'd last seen Grey in their childhood home. Right before Grey had winked out in front of his eyes, just like Rhys had done four days earlier.

"Grey, this is fucking insane. I mean, seriously? Is this real? I mean, look at you."

His brother looked like a Renaissance Faire reenactor, although he probably looked much the same way given the ridiculous outfit he'd put on. But this was no show. The dagger hanging from his brother's belt appeared ominously real.

"It's real." Grey handed him a cup. "Goblet."

Ian blinked.

"The fewer American words you use, the less suspicions you'll raise."

He took the . . . goblet . . . and drank some of the wine, finally getting warm.

"Not bad."

Grey smiled. "That's why I keep wine in here and not ale. The former is actually pretty decent in this time. The latter . . . sucks."

"This time?" he asked expectantly, raising his brow.

Greyson sat on a wooden chair, its leather seat hardly looking fit for the task of holding his brother's frame. But it did, easily.

"Lay it on me." Ian wasn't a fan of mincing words, and Grey knew it.

"The year of our Lord twelve hundred and eighty-six."

At least his brother hadn't lost his sense of humor. "But it's the middle of the winter?"

"Aye. Apparently time isn't linear. How long has it been?"

"Since you've been gone in our world?"

Grey nodded.

"Two weeks."

"Hmmm. I've been here since April."

"April?" Trying to wrap his brain around this flashed him back to his worst subject in school. Math. Ian had despised it. Ask him to give a presentation? He'd ace the assignment. Bullshit a three-page essay? No problem. But black and white answers? He'd never been a fan.

"So time moves slower in the present?"

Grey just shrugged. "Maybe."

"Mom? Rhys? Reik? Your wife? Tell me more." Ian still had a hard time believing their mother was actually alive. That she hadn't abandoned them.

Pulled out of his reverie, Grey leaned over to pour himself wine too. In a *goblet*.

"Mom left a couple of months ago to reunite with Rhys, who's with his wife at—"

"Wait, what?"

Greyson's cocky *I know something you don't* smile had apparently traveled through time with him.

"I have a lot to tell you. We've barely scratched the surface."

"Apparently." Ian downed his wine and poured another, taking a moment to look around the room. It was a lot more colorful than he'd expected. He'd pictured medieval castles as being dark and drab, but perhaps that was just because the surviving tapestries and paintings and such were so old and faded. There was more color here than on a Mardi Gras float.

"Long story . . . very long story short . . . our Aunt Grace consorts with the Fae, who gave her that silver cross and the traveling chant. When Mom was told to deliver a message to the now-dead King Alexander—oh yeah, Mom was a lady-in-waiting to the queen—the king started back to Kinghorn to join his new queen, but before he could ever reach her, his horse was purposely spooked. It lost its footing and fell with the king on it, and both horse and rider died. Turns out it was a setup. I'll spare you the details, but Mom was basically framed for murder. And one of the men tried to kill her too."

He was going to need more wine.

"Mom's sister wanted to save her, so she used the chant to send Mom away. She thought it was just going to send Mom back here to Hightower, but she got one of the words wrong—the devil's in the details—so instead Mom ended up in twentieth-century New Orleans, back when she was only twenty-one. You know the rest."

Ian's mind flashed back to his childhood. His mother's insistence that they learn to ride horseback. Her encouragement of Rhys's fascination with Gaelic. Grey's archery. Her strange, almost melancholy, behavior when they'd visited Scotland. Her disappearance.

His stomach turned at the implications.

"Dad."

His own regret was etched on his brother's face. He'd tried to tell them the truth. So many times.

"Why did he wait so long? Why didn't they both tell us before she disappeared?"

Grey took a sip of wine as if he didn't have a care in the world. Meanwhile, Ian felt panic blast through him. Dad was home, in a New Orleans hospital bed, alone. Jeremy would make sure he was taken care of, but how likely was he to visit?

"And why are you sitting there like a king when Dad is at home dying? Why didn't you try to come back?"

Anger bubbled just beneath the surface, testing his control.

"There's a lot I haven't told you yet, Ian. We're in the middle of a political shitstorm here."

"And why should I give two flying fucks about the political climate? What happens, happens. We know that."

Grey didn't take offense. That was the problem—he never did. Calm as a cucumber.

"Chill, Ian. We didn't have that." Grey nodded to the cross that Ian had put on the small table beside Grey's chair. "Aunt Grace managed to get another one, but she lost it when Yearger, the guy who tried to kill Mom, kidnapped her. And, like I said, we also don't have Rhys, Mom, or Reik."

Ian stared at the cross. It was all just so much . . . too much.

"There are two of those?"

Grey nodded. "When Mom went through time, taking the cross with her, Grace went back to the Fae for help. They gave her a second one as a favor, but they made it pretty clear it was the last one they'd give her."

"So there are two," he repeated.

"Right."

"And Mom and Rhys? Where are they now? Where's Reikart?"

"We've sent word to him at Castle Lochlavine in Liddesdale, to tell him I'm here. But I thought it would be smart for one of us to stay put at Hightower at all times. If we keep running around Scotland looking for each other . . ."

Which was exactly what Ian was doing right now. Running around and looking for Grey. It was a place where Ian had no business getting lost, but he'd never been able to fight his curiosity. The closer he got to the mystery person by the lake, the more the figure came into focus. It was a woman. And she was alone. From the way she was bending down, she appeared to be injured.

He'd only been in the past for a week, but Ian knew enough about the area to liken it to the Quarter. Relatively safe if you knew where you were and didn't venture too far out of your comfort zone. But a few streets in the wrong direction, or in this case, on the wrong person's land . . .

He'd had exactly one week of training with the sword at his side. And after some of the stories Grey had told him, Ian had no desire to meet up with, well, pretty much anyone who wasn't a member of Clan MacKinnish.

This woman might be hurt, however, and she appeared to be alone. He wouldn't ride away from her. She wore a hood, but as Ian came closer, she stood.

Perfection.

There was no other way to describe her. Smooth, slightly pale but in an ethereal way. But her eyebrows and hair were dark. Almost black. And then he did a double take. She looked straight at him, the mark on her left cheek startling him. A birthmark, maybe? It was as big as a plum, although not perfectly round.

Ian had never seen anything like it. Like her. Immediately entranced, he dismounted as she eyed him warily.

Her eyes were also dark, so very opposite from her pale, smooth skin. She didn't say anything. She didn't need to.

He could read her eyes.

I dare you to mock me, they said.

Ian cursed himself for having stared at the mark for too long. Instead, he looked into her chocolate brown eyes.

"Good day," he said, emulating his brother. "My name is Ian MacKinnish."

Her mouth dropped open. But he doubted she was reacting to the good looks and charm that had always served him well with the ladies in his time. No matter how hard he tried, Ian couldn't remember not to use modern terms or sentence structures. And there was nothing to help his American accent.

"Are you okay?"

5

Màiri forgot about her ankle. And the cold. And the fact that she was standing next to a stranger in a place where no one would hear her if she screamed.

She forgot everything but him.

Heart racing, she fought the urge to cover her cheek. Worse, she wanted to touch him, to step forward and cup his strong, smooth jaw in her hands.

What an odd sensation.

He'd asked her something, but she hadn't understood. Or maybe she simply couldn't concentrate. Her focus was too fixed on him—and on the unusual way she was reacting to him.

Chestnut brown hair touched his shoulders, his hair nearly the same length as Ambrose's. But never, not once in all the years she'd known Ambrose, had Màiri felt desperate to kiss his lips, his jaw, his face. Their kiss had been pleasant, but she would have just as soon have continued their discussion.

But this stranger. Ian MacKinnish. She wanted all of those things with him.

Although she'd not heard of an Ian among the MacKinnishes, they were friendly enough with the clan. Perhaps it was foolish of her, but she was no longer afraid, just curious.

Her hand flew to her cheek before she had time to stop it.

Màiri had tried to train herself over the years not to cover the mark she'd been born with, the one that elicited snickers and strange looks. But sometimes it happened when she wasn't thinking.

She dropped her hand, gasping as he took a step toward her.

"I saw you bending down."

If a bear could talk, he would sound that way. His voice entered her ears but settled in her chest. She wanted to hear it again.

"My ankle," she said feebly. "It doesn't hurt any longer."

Which was true. Neither did she feel the cold kissing her cheeks. It was as if this man, this Ian MacKinnish, had brought the summer sun with him. She would be content to stand with him here all day.

Nay, longer than that.

"Glad to hear it."

Still, he didn't move. But his eyes did. They landed exactly where she'd thought they would: on her mark.

Màiri's shoulders sank. "I was born with it."

He did move then, taking off his glove. Standing much too close to be proper, he lifted his hand. And even though Màiri knew what he intended, even though it was so very wrong, she did not wish to stop him.

"May I?"

Nay. Of course you may not. We do not know each other. And even if we did, touching me would be highly inappropriate.

All of that would be true, and yet she found herself nodding.

His hand covered her cheek, the shock of his touch startling her at first. But when his thumb ran across her mark—the mark of the devil, according to the cruelest among them—Màiri did not once consider stopping him.

Nor did she stop him when his thumb moved from her cheek to her bottom lip.

She stood frozen, entranced, as he tugged on it ever so gently.

And then he ran it across her lip, continuing to pull on it until she could actually taste him. This was complete and utter madness. He could rape her as easily as he could seduce her.

"I would never hurt you. Or force you in any way."

How did he know her thoughts?

The stranger closed the remaining distance between them. Màiri had to look up, and gladly did so to keep eye contact with him.

Madness, aye. And yet she did not want to pull away. No part of her wished to do so.

"You are beautiful," he said. "This"—his thumb moved back to her mark—"makes you even more so."

She laughed bitterly.

In response, he lowered his head. He was going to kiss her!

Nay, nay. She could not allow it. This was very, very wrong.

His lips touched hers, hesitant. She opened her mouth just slightly, as Ambrose had instructed, and MacKinnish swept inside. His tongue demanded, and she gave, unsure of precisely how to proceed.

Ambrose had not gone so far.

As the man's thumb continued to caress her cheek, he deepened their kiss. The sensations were new, but Màiri caught on quickly. And despite the madness of kissing a complete stranger out here by the lake, it felt right. Divine, in fact. As if she was meant to be standing here, in the bitter cold, wrapped in the arms of this man who'd called her beautiful *after* he'd seen her mark up close.

This man who didn't shy away from it but touched it, as if it were something lovely.

This man whose lips glided over her own, coaxing and instructing.

When he reached into her mantle and grabbed her waist, she pushed closer. The moan she heard was her own. A strange sound, one she had never imagined would escape her lips.

Passion.

Something she'd never felt with . . . nay, she would not think of him now. As selfish as it was, Màiri would chance God's punishment for a stolen moment with a stranger. Remembering her first urge, Màiri took off her own gloves, both of them, and reached up to grasp his face. In response, and without parting his lips from hers, he moved his hand upward from her waist.

To . . .

Run across her breast. And that's when she knew she really did have to put a stop to this, but not a single part of her wanted that. Especially not as his hand caressed her, squeezing her breast as his tongue insisted on more.

"Jesus Christ, Ian!"

Màiri stepped back so quickly at the epithet she retwisted her ankle. Ignoring the pain, she picked up both gloves and wished she could bury her face in the hood that had fallen down. Quickly pulling it back into place, she looked up to see two men staring down at them.

She did not recognize one, but the other was their neighbor, Ross MacKinnish. At least the stranger had been telling the truth. He did, in fact, appear to be a MacKinnish.

"This isn't The Swamp," said the man she didn't recognize. "What the hell are you doing?"

Swamp?

"I was . . ." Ian looked at her then, as if he was as surprised by what had happened between them as the newcomers. Two dimples appeared in his lower cheeks. Màiri couldn't look away. A few minutes ago he'd been so intense, and now it appeared as if he had not a care in the world. Who *was* this man? "I was looking for you."

Ross cleared his throat. She supposed she should acknowledge him now, though she wished for nothing more than to crawl into the snow. "Good day, Ross."

As if finally remembering the cold, she shivered. The man called Ian moved toward her, but his companion stopped him.

"I don't think so. Move off, little brother."

They were brothers? Now that she knew, they did bear a resemblance. And both of them had that strange accent she could not place.

"Good day, Lady Màiri," Ross acknowledged. She pulled her mantle a little tighter about her body, and his sharp eyes caught the gesture. "Shall we escort you home?"

"Lady Màiri, as in the laird's daughter?" The brother's eyes widened as he looked at Ian. It really did appear as if he wished to kill him.

Màiri curtsied to Ross's companion. "I do not believe we've met."

Ian looked between her and his brother, a small smirk playing on his lips. She suspected she knew what he was thinking—she'd not met either of them before, but she wasn't about to remind the group of that fact. It was shameful enough to have been caught in such a compromising position.

"Greyson MacKinnish. Apologies, my lady, for my brother's boorish behavior."

She glanced at Ian, who did not appear apologetic at all. The opposite, in fact.

"Come, we will escort you back," Ross said.

Before anyone could stop him, Ian moved toward her and fitted his arm around her.

"Your ankle," he whispered before she could mention the inappropriateness of his assistance. No less inappropriate, she supposed, than sharing a kiss with the man or allowing his hand to roam freely across her bodice.

Again, she kept such thoughts to herself.

"Thank you," she said quietly as he helped her mount.

When the handsome stranger walked away to mount his own horse, Màiri had the strange urge to call him back. But that was impossible, of course, and the impact of what had just happened was slowly beginning to dawn on her.

They started back toward the castle, Màiri's thoughts racing. She had never, ever, behaved in such a way before. The kiss with Ambrose had been chaste in comparison, and the only people who knew it had happened were Màiri herself, Ambrose, and Alana. Her deeply religious father would be mortified, or worse, if he learned of her dalliance with the stranger. Certainly he'd not learn of it from her. Would any of the MacKinnish men tell him?

Likely not, she reasoned. They'd spent the past month attempting to convince her father to realign with his former allies. Surely they'd not risk angering him.

They rode in silence, Màiri stealing glances at the handsome man, Ian, when no one else was looking.

Just as they reached the gatehouse, she caught his eye once more. Unlike her, he looked neither ashamed nor apologetic. In fact, he smiled so broadly his dimples appeared again. If she wasn't careful, Màiri would find herself smiling back, which would simply not do.

She would have to ignore him, to pretend she'd not allowed herself to be kissed for the second time in her life. This time, by a man she did not know.

But one who had awoken something inside of her Màiri was afraid would not retreat quietly, even if she willed it so.

6

THIS IS EXACTLY why he hadn't applied to Yale like his brothers, choosing instead to stay in his home state for college. When he was fifty years old, he would still be the little brother. The look Grey gave him now, as they were escorted into the keep, was one he'd seen hundreds of times before. It didn't help that he still lived at home and not across the river with Reik and Grey, but someone needed to keep an eye on dad.

Rhys. Greyson. Reik. His father. They all had one thing in common. That look. He was twenty-seven, but they still treated him as if he were fifteen. And that was being generous.

Grey had only said one thing to him on the ride over—a hissed "keep your mouth shut."

Maybe he had a right to be pissed. After all, Ian was the one who'd insisted he wanted a role in what Grey called *clan politics*. He hadn't liked the thought of sitting around and twiddling his thumbs while his brother and Ross did everything.

And so Grey had given him a job.

"Use your silver tongue to convince the surly laird of Clan Kelbrue to come back to Bruce's side," Grey had said.

Except he'd used his tongue in a very different way, and now the laird might not be inclined to be charmed by him. Which could very well prove to be a problem, if Mom was to be believed.

Mom had passed quite a bit of information along to her brothers before leaving for Lochlavine, including their neighbor's role in the upcoming Wars of Independence. Apparently the laird's son was to become a senior general in the younger Bruce's army, and he would be instrumental in the Scottish victory in the Battle of Bannockburn many years from now. Only problem? The elder Bruce had pissed off the cranky old laird—Grey's words—and their clan was no longer allied with the Bruce family.

Oh, and the fact that Màiri didn't have a brother. Another minor sticking point.

Ian had argued that perhaps their intervention wasn't needed. Wouldn't the future work itself out? Maybe the nonexistent son would join Bruce on his own, despite his father's allegiances? Who were they to interfere?

Ross and Grey had argued they had no way of knowing how time travel worked. Perhaps the McCaim brothers were the ones who'd convinced the laird to realign himself with the Bruces. Or perhaps their very presence would change history.

Ian had argued that point—he'd made the journey last, and his knowledge of events matched up with his brother's, although he'd never paid too much attention to the fine points of history.

Truthfully, he could not give a fuck about any of it. His objectives were simple: reunite with Rhys, Reik, and Mom, use the cross, and get the hell home.

But the same could not be said of Grey. He'd drunk the Kool-Aid, lots of it, and he was clearly not happy. But Christ, this woman. Ian wasn't used to losing control like that, but he was pretty used to taking what he wanted, and he wanted Màiri in the worst way. Too bad he had momentarily forgotten about the whole time travel thing.

"Until later, my boy," he said to his horse. Reikart had always been very insistent they talk to them in order to forge a bond. "My brother would think highly of you for sure."

He stopped, noticing the looks of exasperation directed his way.

A stable boy took their horses, and Màiri led them into the great hall. Although it was approximately the same size as the great hall at Hightower, it was nearly empty. Except for the man sitting in a chair that might have been called a throne if it were more ornate. The simple wooden high-back chair sat on top of the dais. But there were no tables set up for meals. Just the chair. And the man. Others stood off to the side, but one was clearly in charge.

A grizzled-looking, frowning man. He might have been called a *mountain man* back home. With a brown-grey beard and hair to match, he wore one of the belted plaids Grey had told him would someday turn into a kilt. He was nearly as terrifying as some of the MacKinnish uncles, Ross included.

Actually, maybe more. Because for some reason, his brother was nervous. No one else could likely tell, but Ian knew the signs. He watched as Grey flicked his thumb off his forefinger. What the hell was that all about?

His gaze shifted to Màiri as she pulled down her hood. Ian actually stumbled. Like a prepubescent teen. Her hair, nearly black, tumbled around her shoulders in waves. Was she even real?

From the look in her eyes, she was also nervous—even more so than when they'd first met—and she was looking at this man, who had to be her father, as if he were God. Huh. Why was everyone so skittish?

"MacKinnish," the man grumbled at Ross.

"Kelbrue," Ross grumbled back. "My nephews and I came upon your daughter and escorted her home."

"Nephews?"

"Sons of my mother's sister."

It was the story they'd given to everyone but immediate family and those who knew Ian's mother well, as it was impossible to explain how Shona, whom they'd known as a twenty-one-year-old woman, was suddenly a much older woman with three grown sons.

Everyone crossed themselves, the mountain man included. Ian was quick to do the same.

The laird looked at his daughter, who smiled as if she knew she was in trouble. "'Twas just a short ride to the loch."

"Without a guard."

"On our property."

"Bordering theirs."

Theirs? The MacKinnishes? The man's brogue was so thick, Ian could hardly understand him. The daughter's words were easier to follow. Why would that be? He'd noticed the same thing at Hightower: everyone sounded different. But he supposed the same was true of people who were raised in New Orleans—some had thick accents and some did not.

"*He* was not there," Màiri said.

Ian shifted, now wondering who "he" was.

Laird Kelbrue looked at him and then Grey.

"Thank you for returning my daughter safely."

Ah hell. Ian had a bad habit of not being able to lie very well. Or at all. It made for some nasty fights between him and his brothers. As the head of McCaim Shipping's PR team, he had to skirt the line of truth more often than he liked. When he refused to cross it, even just a little, it infuriated pretty much everyone.

"It was our pleasure to do so," Grey said.

The laird looked directly at him then.

Ian, keep your mouth shut. You're supposed to charm this guy, not piss him off.

"I apologize for her behavior," the laird said.

"Father!"

Ian didn't look over at her, but he could imagine that beautiful face twisted in anger, and he didn't blame her. She'd done nothing wrong. Well, not really.

For fuck's sake, would he ever listen to his brother? Probably not.

"I'm the one who should apologize, Laird."

"Ian," his brother warned next to him. Ross's face looked like a thundercloud.

They obviously didn't want him to say anything, but it occurred to him that they'd be a hell of a lot worse off if she told her father about the incident later. Ian would never save face if that happened. Maybe the kiss wasn't the kind of thing she'd tell her dad about, but Ian had always told his mother everything.

No, it would be best to be forthright with the man.

"I did not realize she was your daughter," he started, but his uncle cut him off.

"Ian, my boy," he said, his words full of warning.

The laird held up his hand. "Let him finish."

There was never any shame in the truth. And if they wanted to gain this man's respect and confidence, lying wouldn't be a good start.

Ian held his head high and started again.

"I did not realize she was your daughter when we met." He chose his words carefully, as Grey had taught him. His brother wasn't the only one who could speak as if he were attending a black-tie event. "I was, perhaps, a bit too forward with her. And for that, I do apologize."

"Fuck."

Grey had sworn under his breath, but he'd said the word

loudly enough for Ian to hear. What was he so worked up about?

"*Forward?* Did you compromise my daughter?" The laird leaned forward, eyes flashing.

"Father, 'twas just a simple kiss."

And then all hell broke loose.

Laird Kelbrue stood from his chair, his bellowed "kiss" likely heard by the rest of the MacKinnishes at Hightower. Ross and Grey immediately launched into apologies, and Màiri rushed forward, grabbing her father's arm.

What the hell?

For his part, Ian just hoped the father didn't come at him. The laird was a big guy, but Ian was too. He could beat him easily in a fight, but the last thing he wanted to do was punch out the guy he'd come here to charm.

"What happened at that loch, Màiri?" the laird shouted.

Ian did step forward then. He'd not let her take the blame.

"I kissed her, sir." Cursing at himself for the anachronism, he tried again. "Laird. We'd just met, and I thought your daughter lovely . . ."

Yeah, this wasn't helping. The man's face was so red, he feared he'd given him a heart attack.

"Father, please."

"Did he force himself on you?" the man roared.

All eyes turned toward Màiri, who didn't hesitate to answer truthfully.

"No, Father, he did not. I forgot myself. I . . ."

She looked at him. And boy was she pissed.

So maybe being truthful wasn't always the best approach. The feeling of having messed up royally was compounded when Ross and Grey flanked him, as if preparing for a fight. A literal fight. Judging from all the people who'd suddenly filtered into the back of the hall, it was a fight they would lose.

Shit.

The mountain man narrowed his eyes at Ross, who muttered something under his breath.

"My daughter has been dishonored."

Ross answered before he could. "They shared a kiss, nothing more. We were witness to it."

Technically, they'd gotten to second base, but he didn't blame his uncle for not saying so. The laird already looked like he wanted to kill them.

"He has dishonored my daughter, who has kissed no man before."

His eyes flew to Màiri. From the way she'd opened her mouth for him, he didn't believe it had been her first kiss.

A sense of dread began to creep up his neck. Ian didn't like the energy in the room. He suddenly felt the same way he had five years ago, when Rhys had walked into his bedroom, a blank stare on his face, and said those fateful words: "Mom didn't come home last night."

He held his breath, waiting for the hammer to drop.

"They will marry," Laird Kelbrue said. No, commanded.

If Ian's admission had caused a shitstorm, this was even worse. Màiri pleaded with her father, and although he couldn't hear what she was saying over his uncle's shouting, she was clearly not very happy about the prospect.

Ian wasn't worried. The man was clearly joking.

Wasn't he?

"Grey," he whispered as Ross approached the laird, "what's going on?"

His brother glared at him, his jaw set.

"Why the hell did you tell him?" His hushed whisper made the words no less ominous. Maybe more so.

"What? It was just a kiss. I figured it was better to tell him directly than let him find out some other way."

"This isn't twenty-first-century New Orleans. You don't run around kissing women without any repercussions."

His brother was deadly serious.

"But marriage? It was just a kiss."

"It does seem a bit extreme," his brother admitted. "But the laird is a notoriously religious man, so you might be well and truly screwed."

Everyone in the hall had turned to look at him. What the hell did they want him to say? That he would marry a woman simply because he'd *kissed* her? It was insane.

At least one person was on his side. Lady Màiri looked beyond pissed.

"I would speak with my nephew alone," Ross said, more as a statement than a question. He'd already grabbed his arm like he was some wayward child liable to run to escape punishment. In truth, he was tempted to do just that, although he doubted the people at the back of the hall would let him get very far. The Viking, as Grey fondly called Ross, dragged him to an alcove in the passageway just outside the hall, Grey following them, and then let loose.

"I thought your brother foolish in his dealings with Marian. But this is beyond foolish."

Lady Marian, his brother's wife. Ian still had a hard time believing Grey was married. And not by force. He'd actually chosen such a state. Though Ian had to admit he quite liked the woman, especially given her name. The Robin Hood jokes about his archer brother would be endless now.

"Uncle, this is crazy. Marriage? Over one kiss?"

Ross looked to Grey for help.

"It's like I said, unwed people just don't do that here." He had the decency to look somewhat repentant. "At least, they don't do it the first time they meet, and if they do break decorum, they make sure not to get caught."

"Get caught?" Ross rubbed the back of his neck. "You told the laird of your indiscretion. This is all your doing."

"Indiscretion?" Ian was starting to get hot despite the cold stone wall he'd leaned against. "It was a damn kiss."

But he could see that it wasn't. Not here. Not in this time.

"You don't seriously think I should marry her?"

His brother knew as well as anyone Ian was not prepared to marry.

Ross and Grey exchanged a glance. One he didn't care for at all.

"We need him on Bruce's side." Grey put up his hand, knowing Ian would argue that point. "You have zero chance of helping the situation if you piss him off—" Ross cleared his throat, his typical warning that one of them had said something inappropriate, "—if you anger him further."

Ian waited.

Both of them just stood there, watching him.

He knew what it meant: they actually wanted him to go through with it.

"That's it? That's all you have? You're worried he might be pissed, or angered, or whatever the fuck you want to call it, if I don't marry his daughter? That *maybe* I should do it so I can convince him to return to Bruce's side so *maybe* his son can fight for him to win some battle?"

They had to be kidding.

"Seriously?"

But Ross looked serious as a heart attack. He turned to his brother. "Grey . . ."

His brother cut him off.

"Kissing a woman like Lady Màiri in public, and then telling her father, a laird who's an extremely religious man . . . it's like getting a girl pregnant in our time."

The hair on the back of his neck stood up straight.

Obviously he knew he wasn't in New Orleans anymore, let alone the twenty-first century. He wasn't a total idiot. But kissing a girl and getting her pregnant seemed like completely different things to him.

"Consarn it, ye wee bastard!" The woman's shrill scream was, thankfully, not aimed at him. A woman dressed like a servant stopped short as she chased a young boy around the corner.

"Pardon, my lords."

My lords.

Yup, I'm not in Kansas anymore.

Ian felt the same creeping sense of dread he'd experienced after a shipyard accident last month. The situation had been completely out of his control, yet it had been his job to manage the fallout.

He'd kissed the woman and announced the fact to her father. And if Grey thought this was serious, then it was. Maybe he should play along. Besides, he wouldn't be staying here long. As soon as their family was reunited, he'd be vanishing out of medieval Scotland quicker than a snowball in hell.

God, he could go for a condensed-milk-covered snowball now. And a hot shower.

He'd leave, and Lady Màiri would be "widowed" and free to carry on with whomever had taught her to kiss that way. She'd said, *He was not there.* Had she intended to meet someone at the lake? A secret lover, perhaps? Why else would she have been in the middle of nowhere, alone? He'd been in medieval Scotland for less than a week, and even he knew it was dangerous to ride out alone.

"I've done stupider shit than this," he said, shrugging his shoulders. Well, okay, maybe not quite this stupid, but nevertheless, it looked like he was getting married. At least his wife was hot. Not that he'd be having sex with her.

He hadn't brought any condoms along, and the last thing he wanted to do was leave a kid behind to be raised centuries before he himself was even born.

Time travel could give a guy a headache.

"Only you would smirk about something this serious," his brother said.

If Grey was disgusted with him, it wouldn't be the first time. Ross, for his part, just gave him an odd look and walked away, apparently expecting them to follow.

Tossing his arm around his brother, Ian tried to lighten the mood.

"So talk to me about what they do here for bachelor parties."

7

"THIS CAN NAE BE HAPPENING."

Màiri fingered the deep green gown that had been her mother's. Alana had retrieved the garment and secured a gold chain belt around the waist to give it more shape than had been the custom when it had last been worn.

A gesture Màiri appreciated even if the occasion was not one for celebration.

If the past sennight had been filled with pleas for her father to stop this madness—ones he had disregarded—this day had been the opposite. Resigned, she watched as Alana continued to pack her trunk. The one that would be going with her to Hightower.

A wave of hopelessness washed over her.

"Alana?"

Her voice came out as a squeak. When Alana looked up, she immediately dropped the kirtle in her hands and came to her. Crying on your maid's shoulder the morn of your wedding did not bode well for the marriage. But it was clear she was not going to get out of this match. Ambrose had not come to see her. He had not even sent word back to her.

Nearly frantic to speak with him before today, she'd contemplated stealing away by herself. But her father was being even more watchful than usual, and she doubted she could convince the guards to allow her passage. Besides which, riding to the lake alone was dangerous enough. She wasn't fool enough to attempt riding all the way to Clan Dern.

"Do nae cry, my lady. 'Tis yer wedding day."

Màiri knew it well.

She'd woken up each morning, her stomach swirling and heart heavy. Pulling away and taking the kerchief Alana offered, she wiped her eyes like the expert she now was in drying tears from her face.

Alana took her shoulders more firmly than she had the day before.

"Yer father would never have agreed to see you wed to Ambrose Dern. The feud between our clans runs too deep." Despite her very serious expression, Alana added, "Unlike the loch."

Màiri couldn't help it—a smile tugged at her mouth.

"Two summers," she reminisced. "And the loss of some very good pike."

"Yer father's favorite."

Indeed, it took an angry man to drain an entire loch just to prevent his enemies from fishing in it. The extreme measure proved his enmity toward the former allies.

And yet . . .

"Perhaps he would have . . ."

Alana shook her head. "Nay, lass. I have been trying to tell you. He would not."

Màiri's shoulders slumped, the truth laid bare before her. She felt as if she would be ill.

"But to marry a stranger . . ."

Alana still held her shoulders, and she squeezed them now. Lips pinched together, her maid looked into her eyes. "A stranger with the self-assurance of a king and the countenance of a knight? You may not have been pleased by his admission, but 'twas honorable of him to offer it."

Màiri tended to believe his blurted confession had been more foolish than noble.

"I know him not at all."

"He is a MacKinnish."

Which was the reason, she suspected, her father had insisted on the match. Although her father had withdrawn his support of the Bruces, he'd always liked the MacKinnishes. He'd seen the kiss as an excuse to eliminate the possibility his daughter might marry into Clan Dern. Moreover, she would not be far from home.

Knowing her father's motives did not make them more agreeable.

"He is arrogant," Màiri said.

"But he does not look at you and see yer mark."

Màiri's eyes widened. Alana never spoke of her mark. Ever. When she'd told the maid about the kiss, Màiri had slipped, making mention of the way he'd held his hand on her cheek. It had been a remarkable gesture, but not one she'd thought to share aloud.

She swallowed.

"Ambrose Dern is a good man," Alana said. "And he will make a fine husband for someone who does not love him as a friend."

Màiri froze, surprised to hear her own suspicions being voiced by the woman who knew her heart better than she knew it herself.

"Marriage has naught to do with love," she said.

Alana made a knowing sound, something she'd miss at Hightower. Actually, she'd miss everything about the dear woman, but when her maid had begun to prepare herself for the move, Màiri had stopped her. Her father needed Alana, and she him.

Perhaps they would even admit to their love for each other someday. As much as she wanted Alana to come with her, she couldn't bear to be the person who parted them.

"You didn't say that to your father when you were tellin' him what a fine match ye'd make with Ambrose."

Of course, she was right. But Màiri was not willing to admit it.

"Now, you agreed to this marriage, the banns have been posted, and today is yer weddin' day. So come here and get you prepared."

Aye, she'd agreed, but only because her father had made it clear she had little choice. Not because her heart skipped a beat whenever she thought of that kiss.

Speaking before she could stop herself, she asked what she had been wondering all morn. "Will you tell me, if this must be done, of the marriage bed, then?"

Màiri could feel her cheeks warming as she spoke, but there was no help for it. By nightfall, she would no longer be an unmarried maid . . . unless Ambrose surprised her and did something to stop the wedding from happening. But she'd been waiting several days for him to come, and he had not. Would he be there, at the ceremony? What would she say to him? And he to her?

It would seem the afternoon would be an eventful one, if not entirely pleasant.

45

8

IF IAN HAD EVER BOTHERED to envision his wedding day, it wouldn't have looked like this: standing beside an angry-looking, albeit beautiful woman on the front steps of a chapel in the middle of Scotland. It was no Saint Louis Cathedral. There'd be no second line. But at least one brother was with him to witness what would someday be his *first wedding*, at least to those in the know.

Do you remember that day, Grey would say, *when you royally pissed off that Scottish laird and were forced to marry his daughter?* They would laugh about it. Someday.

But just now it wasn't particularly funny. It was beyond him why they couldn't at least go inside the chapel. Apparently the service that would follow their wedding vows was nothing more than a regular old mass.

They should really make an exception in the middle of winter. It was fucking cold.

A not-so-gentle nudge in his side forced his attention back to the priest. Shit, his bride-to-be had a hell of an elbow. The priest was apparently waiting for some kind of response from him. It would feel a bit rude to ask the old guy to repeat himself.

Before he'd tuned out, the priest had asked Màiri if she accepted the terms, so Ian supposed it was his turn. Hopefully he wasn't agreeing to anything too outrageous.

As if anything was more outrageous than the actual fact that the two of them were standing here, getting married.

"I do."

Another jab. So, not the right answer. What was it Màiri had said?

"Aye, Father. I will."

He would have to ask Grey what "bonny and buxom in bed and at board" meant, exactly. He had caught that bit. Although he could probably guess at the second part on his own, not that it mattered.

There was no kissing the bride. They were practically shoved into the chapel, and Ian wouldn't have even known for sure that he was now married if Greyson and Marian hadn't offered their hearty congratulations.

His brother seemed to be having fun with this now that the initial shock of his foolish actions had worn off. Oddly, he was separated from Màiri, who was escorted to the opposite side of the chapel by her father, who hadn't stopped glaring at him since the start of this—after he'd agreed to the marriage . . . during the negotiations . . . throughout the ceremony. He was angrier than Ian had been in his last fight with his mother.

His chest constricted as it did every time he thought of that morning.

It's okay to leave, she'd told him. *They'll be your brothers whether you work with them or not.*

His knee-jerk reaction had been to think she believed him less capable than the others—she didn't see him as an asset to the family company. Only later, after his temper had cooled, had he realized she genuinely cared about his happiness. Somehow she'd known what no one else seemed to notice: Ian was unhappy in his job.

His position at McCaim Shipping was as corporate as you could get. And he hated everything about it, except for being in business with his brothers.

But he hadn't been ready to admit it, not even to her, and she'd walked out of the kitchen, shaking her head.

It was the last time he'd ever seen her.

"Jesus, Ian. At least try to look less like you're about to jump off the Causeway."

Grey stood up next to him in the uncomfortable wooden pew they'd been herded into. At least this felt familiar.

"She's looking at you."

Ian ignored his brother, already aware of the fact. He could feel her gaze on him.

"*Ian.*"

The priest glanced their way.

"Shhh. You're getting me in trouble in church again," he muttered, trying not to smile. Grey had always had a hard time keeping quiet, particularly during mass.

They didn't talk again, but neither did he look to the other side of the chapel. The few glances he'd seen had been enough. When she'd first approached them, wearing a deep violet, fur-lined cloak like the heroine in a fantasy movie, he'd felt that familiar pull toward her, just like he had by the loch that day. Her gloved hand had risen to touch her cheek, and he'd fought the urge to capture it in his own.

He had to keep reminding himself this wasn't a real marriage. Lady Màiri Kelbrue, daughter of the laird of Clan Kelbrue, was not his real wife. Their arrangement was temporary. And if he wanted it to stay that way, he couldn't let the foolishness of their first meeting happen again.

He didn't need Grey to tell him she was likely a virgin, even if she didn't kiss like one. And that's exactly how she'd remain for her next husband.

Finally, the interminable mass ended and Ian found himself shuffled back outside. He felt rather than saw Màiri as she fell in beside him, her presence like a beacon—one he could not follow. People and horses and carts were everywhere. Where the hell had they come from? There hadn't been this many people in the chapel. Cheers erupted as he and his wife—*wife*, for fuck's sake—walked toward their mounts. Though they'd wed at Kinross, according to their agreement, their wedding reception would be held in their new home. Hightower Castle.

As they accepted the well-wishes, he felt Màiri stiffen next to him. Ian followed her gaze out into the crowd. Some people were already walking away. Others, like his brother, Marian and the laird of Clan Kelbrue, were talking amongst themselves. But one man stood next to a cart, presumably of Màiri's belongings, staring up at them.

Ian knew that look well. The green-eyed monster, like every other emotion, it seemed, had been alive and well for hundreds of years.

The man was about his age, not quite thirty. A good-looking guy. Ian was confident enough that he never hesitated to acknowledge another man's good looks. Màiri's admirer was smaller than him, although not overly so, and had a trimmed dark-blond beard. He also looked like he wanted to kill Ian.

This guy was in love with his wife.

He looked at Màiri, and her expression gutted him. If he was reading this right, she felt the same way. Was this the man she'd arranged to meet that day?

"Go talk to him."

She looked at him as if he were crazy.

"I . . . I cannot. I am a married woman now."

Ian tried not to roll his eyes. If thirteenth-century marriage meant he could no longer even talk to the opposite sex, ever, it definitely wasn't for him.

Actually, he doubted marriage in general was for him, but that was beside the point.

"It looks like he really wants to talk to you."

Hopefully he could tell her sooner rather than later that their marriage was a farce—and she'd be free to marry her lover, or whoever this guy was, before long. He still hadn't figured out how he'd explain the whole time travel thing, but if she didn't believe him, he had Grey and Marian and Ross to back him up.

"Will it help if I come with you?"

That didn't seem to appease her.

"Nay."

In the end, it didn't matter. The lovesick guy approached them directly.

"I offer my sincere congratulations to you, my lady," he said.

A smooth operator, this one.

"Many thanks. Although . . ." She paused. Clearly his wife wanted to say something. But they had an audience now. Several people had gathered around them, watching the exchange with open interest.

These people really needed to stand down. They were acting like superfans at the Super Bowl. When a few of them began staring at Màiri's mark, their interest obvious enough that she lifted her hand to cover it, a surge of protectiveness surprised him.

His training kicking in, Ian handled the situation as he would have approached it back home. No one would stare at his wife like she was some carnival sideshow act. Grasping her elbow, he urged her forward while speaking to Lord Lovesick.

"Too much attention. If you come to Hightower, I'll arrange for you to speak privately there."

Ian didn't wait to catch the guy's reaction. He made swift work of helping Màiri mount her horse and then climbed atop his own mount. If only he'd spent more time with Reik riding. Without glancing back at the crowd, he nodded to Ross and his new father-in-law, both of whom were already mounted and probably getting impatient, to signal they were ready.

It took him a while to notice his wife's expression. She was looking at him like, well, maybe like he was from another century. Because he was. And it was time she learned all about it.

9

AMBROSE WAS HERE in the hall, dining with the other wedding guests.

When her new husband had offered the invitation, Màiri had not expected him to accept it. Especially not this evening. But as her father and Ross MacKinnish toasted their renewed alliance—part of the marriage agreement—she noticed him at the very back of the hall. Wouldn't the laird of Clan MacKinnish be surprised when he returned. She'd heard he had been away but was due to arrive back home soon.

Màiri had eaten the meal mostly in silence. She was seated on the dais next to her new husband, Grey, Marian, and Ross. It was difficult to believe she was now wed, her dream of marrying Ambrose gone. And he'd never even come to her until it was over.

"There's no need to cover it," he said, the remark delivered in his deep, husky voice.

Màiri pulled the pewter wine goblet toward her. She'd never drunk more than two at one time before, but this felt like the perfect occasion to do so.

"'Tis a habit." She hadn't even realized she'd done it this time.

"It's beautiful."

Her heart leapt at his words, but she dismissed the sentiment. Surely her mark was anything but. She had seen it more than once in her reflection on polished brass. And had lived with odd looks from strangers that proved otherwise.

"I'm not kidding. It's unique, a part of you. And you are a beautiful woman, Màiri."

Màiri. He spoke her given name as if they were familiar. Which was perhaps the right of it. They were married now.

"Many thanks"—she tried out his name on her lips as well —"Ian."

Màiri leaned forward to look at her father sitting on the other side of Ross MacKinnish. He was glancing at her too, and although she could not discern his expression, it lacked any heat. Truthfully, after that first day, he'd acted more relieved than upset. He despised Clan Dern that much.

When she looked back at Ian, he was staring at her, his eyes like liquid gold. Piercing. That he did not look away made Màiri want to, but she held his gaze instead. Reminded of their meeting less than a sennight before, she felt her cheeks grow warm.

"That look is what got us into this mess."

Even though she agreed the situation was indeed a mess, Màiri hated to hear the words aloud. This was certainly not what she had envisioned for her wedding day.

"I look at you as I would any man."

"Ha!"

She should be offended by his laughter, but instead she found herself smiling.

Ian leaned closer to her. "You father said I was the first man you've ever kissed, but I know that isn't true."

Màiri's back straightened. "You accuse me of being loose? 'Tis a fine way to begin a marriage."

His expression changed in a way she didn't understand. She

narrowed her eyes. "Where are you from that your manner of speech is so brazen?"

He took a sip of wine as if giving himself more time to answer her question. Did he not know from where he hailed?

"I am from many places," he finally said, "the most interesting one being here, in this very moment."

It was not much of an answer, and they both knew it. What was he hiding? Màiri knew only that he was the son of Laird MacKinnish's sister-in-law. So why had he never been to Hightower before? For the two clans were close enough that she would have heard of the man if he'd made a previous visit.

"You did not answer my question," she pressed.

Musicians played as the guests finished the final course of the meal. But Màiri could not revel in the celebratory atmosphere of the evening. She could barely eat a bite. Finally, she stopped resisting and looked into the crowd. Ambrose was watching them, just as he had been when last she'd looked.

"Ahh. So he's the one you've kissed?" Ian whispered. "I wondered."

She looked at her husband sharply. "'Tis not proper to discuss."

"I am now wed to you because your father believes our indiscretion was your first. So yes, it is a proper topic of discussion."

Màiri decided not to comment.

"Who is he?"

She frowned. "Ambrose . . ."

It was as far as she got before Ian choked on his wine.

"Ambrose? Seriously? Sounds like my brother's Yale friends."

None of which meant anything to her, although she understood he was making a jest. At her friend's expense. Màiri glared at him, and he pressed his lips together in an apparent attempt to stop laughing.

"'Tis a fine name," she countered.

"And I'm sure he is a fine man."

Somewhat pacified, as he seemed sincere, she answered, "He is indeed a fine man. We've been friends since childhood and planned to marry."

"So why didn't you?"

Màiri glanced at her father.

"Ahhh. I see."

Ian's brother said something to him then, and Màiri was left to observe the great hall of Hightower Castle. She'd not visited the castle for over a year, and there were subtle changes it had taken her a while to notice. Fresh rushes, scented too. And it appeared all of the tapestries had been cleaned, their bright colors more vibrant than she remembered. Bronze and silver gleamed from every table. Although not known for their excesses, Clan MacKinnish was wealthy. Their close connection to Clan Bruce had increased their influence.

Even when her father had been allied with the Bruce, he'd never been particularly taken with the man. Over the years he and the elder Bruce had seemed to disagree on more than they did not. The recent attack on Balliol land had infuriated him, so much so that he still had not agreed to renew his support.

Màiri tried to avoid Ambrose's gaze, but she could feel him looking at her.

"Do you love him?"

Would his intimate questions never cease? Màiri's answer was swift. "Aye, I love him."

And yet, she could not prevent herself from thinking of what Alana had said—that her love for Ambrose was that of a dear friend. There was no denying his kiss had not made her feel the same way her husband's had.

"You're dangerous, Màiri."

She glanced up to see Ian looking straight at her again.

"Pardon?"

"I'll explain more later. In the meantime, I promised you a talk with your friend. Go. Everyone is too drunk to notice."

She stared at him incredulously. What sort of man pushed his new wife toward another, particularly on their wedding night? One who cared little for her. Of course, they'd just met. But something about it rankled.

Still, she very much wished to speak to Ambrose. To ask why he'd not come sooner, when something might have been done to prevent the marriage.

"You are sure?"

Ian smiled so broadly, the two indentations in his cheeks appeared.

An odd sensation overtook her, and she forgot precisely what they had been discussing.

"Dangerous," he repeated, though she had no notion of what he meant.

Remembering what they'd discussed, what he'd agreed to, she stood and placed her goblet back onto the table. Then, thinking of what was to come this night—her talk with Ambrose and the wedding bed—she snatched it back up.

The sound of her husband's laughter echoed all the way through the hall.

"HOLD UP."

It took every bit of self-control not to groan at the sound of his brother's voice behind him in the passageway. After her annoyingly long conversation with Lord Lovesick, conducted at the back of the hall, he'd watched his wife leave the hall with her maid. Apparently the maid wasn't here to stay—she hadn't been expected to come at all, but she'd appeared in the hall just before the meal, much to his wife's surprise and delight.

Grey's wife had a few more concerns, it seemed, although she'd refrained from voicing them. He liked his sister-in-law. A lot. But he got the distinct feeling his attitude toward this marriage grated on her even though she hadn't said a word about it. She did follow Màiri out of the hall, and he was glad his wife had someone nice looking out for her.

"Who is he?" his brother asked.

"Who?" he asked, pretending not to know.

Ian shivered, the feeling of standing in the middle of a dark corridor surrounded by wall torches something he'd never get used to. The castle tours they'd taken on their vacation to Scotland had made the buildings seem so remote, unused. Even the rooms that had been furnished to recreate some scene from the past didn't come close to the real thing. It was the people, he realized. History couldn't truly be recreated without them.

"You know who. The guy in the back of the hall talking to Màiri. The one you stared at like he was a king cake."

He laughed. "Ugh. I hate them."

Them being every king cake in existence. A natural reaction given he'd almost choked on one when he was young. If his mother hadn't successfully administered the Heimlich, he might not be here right now. Death by a plastic baby Jesus. Talk about irony.

"Ian, I know it's been a hell of a ride since you got here."

An understatement.

"But this is her real life. Lady Màiri isn't playacting."

Which was precisely what Marian had been trying to convey to him without outright saying it. Leave it to Grey to hit it home.

"No shit."

Grey didn't even flinch.

"And I know you're planning to leave her here if we can get back home, but . . ."

"*When.* When we get back home. I have the cross. Mom, Rhys, and Reikart are all here. Somewhere. And as soon as they hightail it back to Hightower, we're outta here."

"Without your wife?"

"Jesus, Grey. This isn't like you and Marian. I hardly know the woman. Besides, she's in love with that guy. The son of some neighboring clan. The nicest thing I can do for her will be to leave her here, in the *real life* she knows with a man she loves."

"But you clearly like her."

So that's what this was about. Greyson had taken up their mother's torch—trying to fix Ian and make him happy.

"She's hot, for sure."

Grey's eyebrows rose.

"There's something about her. I don't know. But it doesn't matter. This isn't going to be a real marriage, and I'm going to tell her why."

"Not tonight you aren't."

"Why not? She needs to know. Don't you think stringing her along would be a dick move?"

They'd kept their voices down, although from the distant sound of merriment in the hall, the party wasn't going to end anytime soon. Arrangements had been made for Ian and Màiri to stay in a separate tower, different from where he'd been this past week in the main keep. Now that they were a married couple and all that jazz.

"At least wait until you can talk to the father a bit more. For all his blustering, he's genuinely thrilled about this alliance, and with your powers of persuasion, I really think you could bring him back to Bruce's side. Then you can tell her, give her time to adjust. We knew Dad our whole lives, and none of us believed him about the time travel thing. She'll think you're nuts. You know that, right?"

The question hung around them like cemetery fog. Had he been more superstitious, Ian might have said something about the torch that had just extinguished behind his brother's head. His mother had always believed in signs. God knows how she would have read into that expired flame, but she would have. Ian had no doubt of that.

He shrugged, not wanting to dwell on their dad and how shitty he felt for having doubted him.

"Too bad I left my phone on Dad's desk."

Grey's had made it through time intact. He'd used it to take a picture of Marian, which had gone a long way toward convincing her of the truth, but the battery was obviously long dead. And unfortunately, as much as he and Reik had thought their plan through, the only items he'd brought from the future were some scraps of paper with names and a map. Plus a pack of matches, just in case they landed in the middle of nowhere and needed to start a fire. They'd avoided bringing more in order to avoid accusations of witchcraft, but it had left him with no way to prove his wild story. Still, he'd show her what little he'd brought. Call on the others to back him up. It was certainly no slam dunk like a cell phone. He had to try, though. What choice did he have other than to make her believe him?

"She'll expect a wedding night," he said, rubbing his cheekbone.

"So? Give her one."

His eyes widened. "Get her pregnant and then leave? Great plan, Grey."

"I never said to get her pregnant. Or have sex with her. But you can still give her a wedding night. She'll be nervous. Tell her you can take it slow."

He shook his head. "Nope. Not doing it."

When Grey opened his mouth to protest, Ian stopped him.

"Have some faith in me, for once. If you want me to wait a few days before talking to her, see what I can do with the father, fine. But I'm not touching my wife. All of this happened because of a kiss. I'm not going to make things worse."

"Hmm."

Ian was about to walk away, but he could tell Grey wasn't finished.

"What?" If his tone was clipped, he wasn't sorry.

"I'll never understand you, Ian. You're a total jerk in some ways, and honorable to a fault in others. I can't stand you sometimes, but I love you, brother."

He hadn't expected that. If the torch behind his head hadn't gone out, maybe Ian would have known for sure, but he could swear he saw a watery gleam in Grey's eyes. Damned if he'd let that happen to him.

"Same," he said, walking off but smiling to himself.

It was good to have at least one of his missing family members back. Even if he did want to strangle him sometimes.

The thought of strangling someone summoned the image of Lord Lovesick's face, but Ian pushed it back out. He had no beef with the guy. If Màiri wanted to marry him when he left, more power to her.

Ian didn't care. She was his wife in name only.

Now he had to keep it that way.

"You've no need to look so frightened, lass," Alana said. "With a man such as he, 'tis bound to be a pleasurable experience."

Màiri looked back and forth between her maid and Lady Marian. When Greyson's wife had knocked on the door, she'd thought for a wild moment that it was him. That Ian had already come for her. Relieved to see it was not, she'd welcomed her new sister-in-law into the beautifully appointed bedchamber. They sat in front of the hearth, one in each of the lovely chairs, and Alana sat on the large canopied bed behind them.

Before this eve, Màiri had only seen Lady Marian once before, standing beside Greyson at the marriage ceremony. They hadn't spoken at the meal, as they'd been seated on opposite ends of the trestle table. Which was why Màiri was a bit surprised by her sudden visit. It felt strange to discuss such intimate matters around a stranger, but perhaps it wasn't so odd given she'd just married one.

"Your maid is correct," Lady Marian said. "'Tis the reason I came. We've little time to talk as this all happened so fast."

Màiri practically snorted and then covered her mouth with her hand.

Marian's soft chuckle, not judging but understanding, helped ease the situation. She did seem rather kind, and Màiri was grateful she'd have the companionship of another young person here at the castle.

"I've not known Ian for long," Marian admitted. "But as his brother's wife, I can tell you a bit about their family, if you'd like. And I will gladly answer any questions you may have."

Màiri glanced at Alana, who stood from the bed.

"I will pardon myself." Before she left, she walked toward the hearth and leaned down to hug Màiri, who squeezed her tightly.

"You will not leave Hightower just yet?"

"I will leave when you are ready for me to do so."

Màiri really did wish for Alana to remain with her father—they deserved happiness, if only they'd allow themselves to find it—but selfishly she wished her friend would stay.

"I can tell you will miss her," Marian said when the wooden door clicked closed. "Why is she not staying here at Hightower?"

Màiri pulled the fine robe Alana had brought with them tighter across her chest. The fire raged in front of them as if it knew the harsh winter threatened another snowfall. "My mother died when I was just eight. And though she's like a mother to me, I suspect my father needs her more. 'Twill be lonely for him without me, I fear."

Marian stood, making her way to the sole table in the room. Intricately carved and painted bright blue, it stood in stark contrast to the whitewashed stone walls. Using the pitcher of wine Alana had brought in earlier, Marian filled two goblets and handed one to Màiri.

"Nay, I have had three already."

But Marian did not move.

"I should not drink to excess."

A smile tugged at the other woman's lips. "Aye, you should. Take it."

Her father had not been pleased when she'd accepted that

third goblet—she'd seen him glance at her from farther down the table—but he was not in this chamber. And so she took it.

"'Tis kind of you to forgo your maid for your father's happiness." Marian returned to her seat and took a sip of her wine. "I, too, was raised without a mother. She died giving birth to me."

Màiri's eyes widened.

"But unlike the love you and your father clearly have for each other, my father only cared for the allegiance he could make with my wedding."

"Surely he loves you."

But Marian's face told another story. A sad one she suddenly wished to hear.

"We have much time to share tales, but your husband may be coming any time. Ask, and please do not be shy."

Màiri's heart thudded in her chest.

"I did not expect to be married today."

Marian laughed. "I should think you did not, having met Ian just a sennight ago. I am sorry for the circumstances of your wedding, but I can assure you that Ian is a good man, even if I suspect he may not be handling the suddenness of this well. From what Grey has told me, they have a close and caring family."

"Grey," she repeated, never having heard such a strange name.

"'Tis what his family calls him. And you are family now. Please use my given name as well."

The other woman's kindness was exactly what Màiri had needed. Without thinking, she lifted her hand to her cheek. But instead of commenting on the mark or staring at it, Marian took another sip of her wine.

"As your maid said," Marian continued, "'twill be a pleasant experience, I am sure. The McCaim men are not like—" She stopped abruptly.

"McCaim? I thought Ian was a MacKinnish."

"He is, though his father's family are called McCaim. You've heard of them?"

Màiri nodded. "Balliol allies?"

"Aye."

His father's family. McCaim. Odd. And from Marian's expression, she could tell there was something else, something more the other woman wished to say. Another knock at the door prevented her from asking.

"Quick, 'tis likely Ian," Marian said. "Do you wish to know anything more?"

"A moment please," she called out for his ears. "Aye," she added in an undertone. "Will it hurt? Alana could not answer me that question."

"Nay. Or very little." Marian stood, and Màiri followed suit. "You may trust me, Lady Màiri—"

"Màiri, please."

Marian placed her goblet down on the table, but not until after taking a long, appreciative sip. At that moment, Màiri liked the woman, now her sister-in-law, very much.

"You have nothing to fear, Màiri, I promise it," Marian said. "In fact, you will enjoy the intimacies between husband and wife"—she smiled—"very much."

Another knock.

"You can trust me."

Marian strode to the door. Looking back, she gave one final reassuring nod and then opened the door. As expected, Ian stood on the other side.

You looked at him in a way you've never once looked at me.

Màiri had denied it, of course. Although it didn't matter anymore. It couldn't. Ambrose had not wished to anger her father, and she could not blame him. Alana was right after all—he never would have yielded. Besides, she knew in her heart that Ambrose was right. She had never looked at him that way, and her stomach had never fluttered when he was near. Not like it did around Ian.

She loved Ambrose, aye. But she desired her husband.

And Màiri was not so stubborn as her father to deny it.

11

He had loved a woman once.

After Reik's car accident, when his girlfriend had been killed, his brother had been in a bad place. Was still in a bad place, really. So Ian had booked the vacation for them on a whim and forced his brother's ass to Turks and Caicos for a long weekend. Reikart had come back with a tan and a few dozen or more beers under his belt.

Ian had come home with a new long-distance relationship.

Lisa was an account executive from Manhattan. Smart, successful, and driven, but fun-loving too. Although it had started off as a fling, he'd fallen hard for her, and she'd agreed to try long distance—if *he* made the effort. She'd accepted his gifts, urged him to take her on expensive trips, and then she'd left him. Said the long distance was too much. Pics of her new boy toy surfaced on her Instagram account less than a week later. His brothers, never fond of Lisa, had been all too happy to show him. This guy apparently had a house in the Hamptons. And Lisa loved the Hamptons.

She was the only woman he'd ever said *I love you* to, and

she'd broken his heart. After everything went down, Ian had lain awake at night trying to imagine what his mom would have said about the whole thing. Excitement fluttered in his stomach at the realization he could finally ask her. They said time heals all wounds, but it had never healed this one: he missed his mother.

Truth was, he didn't really need to ask what she would have thought of Lisa. He was pretty sure he knew.

But what would his mom have to say about his wife? She'd like her, for sure. What wasn't to like? Beautiful. Kind. Thoughtful. Unfortunately, he wouldn't be here long enough to find out.

The door opened.

He hadn't been expecting Marian.

"I promised her pleasure, not pain. Do see that you give it to her."

He didn't even have time to react to that one before his sister-in-law walked away. *Damn, girl.* No wonder Grey had fallen so hard for her. That kind of loyalty to a woman she'd just met that day . . . Marian had just gone up another notch in his eyes.

Unfortunately, he wouldn't be able to follow through.

If he'd not already tasted Màiri, this whole thing might have been a bit easier. But as he walked inside the bedchamber, Ian knew two things simultaneously.

One, if he stayed here, he'd be hard-pressed to keep his hands off her.

Two, he had never actually been in love with Lisa.

Ian had desired her, sure. Her confidence had attracted him. He'd always loved women who held their heads high, marching into a room as if they owned it and he was merely leasing it from them. But he'd never once felt this kind of pull to the Manhattan gold digger.

Màiri had no idea how beautiful she was, as trite as that might sound. It was no humblebrag for her to hide her face.

How was that possible? Didn't this Ambrose guy worship the ground she walked on? Whatever the case, she had convinced herself she was undesirable . . . which made him want to prove the opposite to her. It was the least he could do before he abandoned her.

"I guess you don't need this." He held up the pitcher of wine he'd brought as he walked toward her. Placing it next to the other, he poured himself a glass, although it wasn't a glass, of course, so much as a goblet. Is that what they said in this time? *Care for a goblet of wine?*

Ian smiled at his own joke.

"You smile a lot."

Not the worst accusation he'd ever heard.

"There's usually a lot to smile about."

Until there wasn't. Mom's disappearance. Dad's sickness. Time travel. His wedding. But Ian would take joy where he could find it. Always had.

He was currently standing in front of a warm fire with a goblet of wine in his hand and a beautiful woman next to him. If not for the circumstances, there would be a hell of a lot to smile about right now.

Stunning. That was the best way to describe Màiri. And seductive too, without having a damn clue about her allure. Her robe, or whatever it was called, wasn't one of the big, fluffy ones you'd find in a hotel. It was thin, highlighting every luscious curve as if to taunt him.

"Shall we sit?"

Seeing the tension ease from her shoulders, he sat down next to her. The padded wooden chair was comfortable, though it was no recliner. He lifted his wine for a toast.

"To an eventful day."

They drank. Ian had a pretty high tolerance, but this stuff was a bit more potent than he was used to, and it was definitely affecting him. He was more relaxed than he'd expected to be on the day he'd been forced to take a wife.

"Smiling again," she said softly.

"This isn't the worst way to spend an evening. Sitting by the fire with a beautiful woman."

He hadn't meant the words to sound facetious, but Ian could see that's how she took them.

"Màiri, I don't plan on consummating our marriage tonight."

Or ever.

That got her attention.

"We hardly know each other. And I'm sorry for how everything—" He nearly said *went down*, but suspected it would earn him a blank look. "How everything progressed. I should not have kissed you. And I probably shouldn't have told your father about it."

"Probably?"

Ian stretched his legs out in front of him.

"I underestimated the force of his response. But I didn't want him to learn of it without me fessing up first."

Màiri, still on the defensive, looked at him over the rim of her goblet as she sipped her wine. If she was thrown by his use of *fessing*, she didn't say so.

"Why?" she finally asked.

Damn Grey. This is the part where he should tell her everything. Show her the documents, not that they were proof of anything, but paper hadn't yet been invented here. And Grey, and Marian, and even Ross could help convince her of the truth.

Then he could just tell her why it had been so important for them to marry. *I didn't want to risk pissing your father off to the point of no return. Your brother is a key part of a battle to come, and your dad needs to realign with Bruce.*

He could still do it. Just because his brother had told him not to . . .

69

"It felt like the right thing to do," he said, because it was true. "If I thought he'd demand that we marry . . ."

Màiri sighed. "You could not have known. He's said many times a stronger alliance with MacKinnish would be desirable, other than the issue of the Bruce. And it also meant that I could not marry Ambrose . . . "

"Your father really hates him that much?"

When Màiri stood to place her presumably empty wine goblet on the table, he bolted up and refilled it instead. She was still a bundle of nerves, and another drink wasn't the worst idea.

She allowed him to do so, standing much too close for his sanity. He could smell her, just like he'd been able to at the meal. Lavender. Not a scent he'd cared much for before, but he was changing his mind on that one.

His breeches tightened at the thought of how easy it would be to slip off her clothes and continue the kiss that had brought them here. To show his wife more pleasure than she'd known possible.

But that didn't fit in with his plans, so he handed her the goblet and quickly sat back down. The way she was looking at him indicated their closeness was affecting her too. Which made it pretty damn difficult to hold back.

"They were allies once."

Bring it back, Ian. Deep breaths. Ambrose. She's talking about Ambrose.

"My father and his. That's how we became friends. And then the Battle of Craigmore between two other northern clans tore them apart. My father refused to fight, not wanting to choose one ally over the other, and the laird of Clan Dern took his refusal as a personal insult."

"And so it began?"

Màiri nodded. "I'd never thought of Ambrose in that way before, as a husband. But he was always a dear friend, and when we happened upon each other after our clans' separation, he mentioned the possibility. And of course I thought it a good plan. But my father did not."

Okay, so this was interesting.

"You never thought of him in that way? As a husband?"

"No."

He knew he shouldn't press, not when he didn't plan to stay married to her, but he couldn't resist. Leaning forward, he watched her eyes as the light from the fire danced across them. She might lie, but her eyes would not.

"When you kissed me back . . ."

He should stop. He could tell from the way she flinched that the topic made her uncomfortable. But he couldn't stop, not now.

"The feelings you had at that moment. Have you felt that way about Ambrose? Ever?"

Ian wasn't surprised at her gasp, but he wasn't going to let up.

"You can tell me anything, Màiri. Even things you've never spoken aloud before. I will never repeat what you tell me to anyone. Nothing, not even your deepest, darkest, most wicked thoughts are off-limits between us."

Of course she didn't believe him.

What the hell. He would never see her again in a few weeks. "My mother coddled me, and I loved it. But I got away with murder too. To the world, I am as confident as my brothers, but they'll always see me as the baby. That's one of the reasons I can't tell them that I hate the position they've given me in the family business. Truth is, I desperately wish I could do something else. On my own. But I can't bring myself to tell them. I'm afraid of feeling useless. Left out."

There. A deep, dark thought he'd never shared with another living person. Not even his mother. She'd picked up on the way he was feeling, but he'd essentially denied it. If he recalled correctly, he'd said something along the lines of, *Not everyone loves their job. So what?*

His words seemed to resonate. Màiri drank deeply from her cup and leaned forward too, her body's defensive posture giving way to a more trusting one.

"Nay. I've never felt anything like that with Ambrose."

He fucking knew it.

"You said I must have been kissed before, and 'tis true. But it only happened once, with Ambrose. And it felt nothing like that day you kissed me."

Well, ask and you shall receive. But now he was well and truly screwed.

His wife's feelings for Lord Lovesick were a sisterly sort of affection, only she didn't know because she'd never experienced true desire. An interesting turn of events. He felt slightly less like punching the guy in the face. Even if he was the asshole who'd encouraged their heart-to-heart.

Now what?

"So, I think I'm gonna need another wine."

***

IAN HADN'T MENTIONED Ambrose again, even after two more wines. Neither did they talk of kissing or feelings, which was just as well. Màiri was afraid she might say too much.

"Tell me about Alana."

This was an easy topic for her to discuss. "She's been like a mother to me. Some think it strange, our relationship. And others begrudge her for acting more like parent than servant. I think it sorrowful that it should matter. But it does, very much."

She told him of the times Alana helped her, guided her. Of the burgeoning feelings between Alana and her father. When she finished, they both turned to the fire. Watching. Listening to the crackle. The silence between them somehow just as comfortable as their discussion.

"You're easy to talk to," Ian said finally.

She's been told the same before and had an answer for it. "This mark"—she gestured upward—"has taught me many things. One is that every person's scar, whether seen or not, weighs on them. I try very hard to remember that."

He stared so intently, Màiri finally looked away.

"You accept others so easily." Ian had a strange look about him suddenly. "What do you think of the Fae?"

She was not prepared for the question. But answered anyway.

"My father, of course, forbids discussion of anything condemned by the church. But Alana"—she smiled—"perhaps their disagreement on so many subjects is part of their reluctance. And they disagree on that one, very much."

"She believes in them?"

"Oh, very much. As I do. Years after I injured my ankle, I twisted it walking through the courtyard one day. On nothing, actually. Just twisted it again while walking. A woman appeared before me who I'd never seen before. Or since. Suddenly, I had the oddest sensation. Never before or since did my body fill with both cold and warmth at once. She smiled, looked toward my foot, and placed her hand on my shoulder. 'You are most kind, my lady,' were the only words she spoke. And then she walked away. It was as if my ankle had not been twisted. For many years it did not bother me again until . . ."

A look passed between them as they both remembered that day. The one they met.

"I'd never have told my father, but Alana agreed that she was likely Fae. Why she came to Kinross, or why she healed me, I cannot say. But never would I presume not to believe what I cannot explain."

Ian opened his mouth, then promptly closed it.

He had been about to say something, but Màiri would not know what his next words might have been. His eyes hooded suddenly, and all thoughts of Alana and Fae fled her mind. Where moments ago their conversation had come easily, now a very different feeling settled over her.

'Twould be a long night indeed.

DESPITE A RAGING case of blue balls, Ian was in his element.

Sure, he and his dad had hunted in much warmer weather, and yeah, they'd typically used guns instead of crossbows, but he'd hunted more than all of his brothers combined. It felt good to be out here in the wilds, deer hounds barking.

"Over there."

Màiri's father pointed, and he saw it. A deer, in perfect position.

They'd been at it all day, keeping themselves low and the red deer upwind. Each of them dismounted, moving quietly into position. His uncle Colban waved him over, away from Grey, who was already preparing his crossbow, and Ross, who'd fallen in with him. Ian didn't know Colban well, but according to Grey, he was basically a mini Ross. Two years younger, slightly smaller, and just as gruff.

"This is a better shot," he said in a brogue as thick as his brother's. "Ross knows less about killing deer than he does about bedding women."

Good to know he and his brothers weren't alone in their friendly, not-so-friendly competition.

"If Grey gets a good shot, we don't stand a chance."

Ian was becoming used to strange looks whenever he used a modern phrase. But he couldn't help it. Even Grey, who had been here for months, slipped up every so often.

"Ross said his bow's aim is true. But they'll spook 'em before they get the chance to fell 'em."

Ian was inclined to agree. They'd hardly covered their scent. Bow ready, he waited in silence, silently willing their prey to approach. A good waterproof jacket and boots would have been nice right about now. The snow was more than knee-deep in places. For that reason alone, he could never stay here. Ian vowed never to complain about Louisiana's mugginess again.

Crouching in a sheepskin cloak on a bed of snow was hardly comfortable, but it was much more so than his sleeping arrangements the night before. After sitting up late with Màiri, exchanging childhood stories with her—his tales tweaked to hide as much of the modernity as possible—they'd gone to bed.

When she'd removed her robe, the thin nightgown—shift—beneath it left little to the imagination. He'd undressed quickly, leaving on more than he normally would, and said goodnight to his flustered-looking wife.

And proceeded to lay there, awake, hard as a rock. Grey had suggested that he pleasure her but leave her a virgin, but that plan had one key flaw.

One taste would not be enough.

Colban's nod drew him back into the present moment. Consumed with thoughts of Màiri, he had almost missed his chance to bag the deer. Colban lowered his bow, signaling the shot was his to make.

Impress Màiri's father. Bring him to our side.

He waited for the red stag to turn ever so slightly. When it did, Ian let the arrow loose. His prey didn't stand a chance. The animal went down cleanly. Standing, he accepted the others' cheers, grateful for at least one aspect of being a medieval nobleman: he didn't have to fetch and clean the deer. He and his dad, and whatever brother went with them, had always had to drag deer from the thick of the Louisiana woods back to their truck.

Soon, he was mounted and riding back toward the castle, his mood more jovial than it had been all day. Fresh meat for all. That salted crap that obviously wasn't refrigerated wasn't his favorite part of the thirteenth century.

"Well done," said the very man he'd hoped to speak to on this hunt, riding alongside him. "You've hunted many times before."

"Aye." He sounded ridiculous, but Laird Kelbrue didn't flinch. It was a start. "I'd like to apologize, my lord, for my actions that led to this day."

It wasn't the first time he'd apologized to the man, and it probably wouldn't be the last.

Kelbrue grunted. "I've no doubt Màiri will be provided for."

The laird clearly wasn't letting him off the hook, but he'd call it progress and take the compliment.

"She will indeed," he said, although it wouldn't be in the way her father expected. The only way to leave without infuriating the man was to fake his own death. She'd be his widow, treated as family by the MacKinnishes, and everyone would say Grey and Marian had left Hightower in grief. Only one person would know the truth: Màiri. Indeed, the sooner Ian told her the truth, the better. In an ideal world, they could explain the situation to her father too, to avoid the ruse, but too many people already knew, and no one understood the implications of their actions here in the past.

"Ross has told me that you've spent more time on the road than in one place?"

This is where he'd have to skate away from the truth a little, no matter how hard it was for him, and *deflect, deflect, deflect.*

"Aye, he is correct. But you . . . you've been here for three generations?"

Thankfully, the laird didn't seem to take offense to the change in topic. Hearing riders approaching, Ian turned to see Grey and Ross closing in. When he turned back in his seat, he took in the magnificent sight of snowcapped mountains in the distance. This place was unlike any he'd ever seen, and suddenly he felt sad for his mother. To be taken from such beauty, dumped in a different time . . .

"My grandfather came here from the north."

As if they weren't north enough. Imagine the weather.

"Were you always allied to my family?"

"Aye. Though we've disagreed many times too. Good men, MacKinnish."

He didn't say it, but *not like Clan Dern* was just on the tip of Ian's tongue. That wasn't where he needed to steer their conversation, though—he had to focus on talking up Bruce, not talking down Ambrose.

"Ross says it's important to keep your allies close, now more than ever. These are interesting times we're in."

He got only a grunt in response.

"You don't agree?"

Màiri's father scowled in response. A tough nut to crack indeed.

"When they're loyal," he finally said.

So that was his Achilles' heel: he believed in loyalty. It was something they could agree on.

"There is no greater quality in a man," he said, firmly and with conviction.

More silence. At which point most would jump to fill the gap with conversation. But Ian had been trained, both in public relations and in sports, to do otherwise. To read body language. To listen. Not to fill the silence with his own words.

"'Tis a shame not all agree with you," Kelbrue said.

Please let him be talking about Bruce.

"I should think my clansmen feel the same way," Ian said.

Kelbrue looked thoughtful. And it struck Ian that the man was riding around in the snow, in the middle of the winter in Scotland, without a hat or gloves. He was a beast.

"We may be allies, but we disagree about many things."

Ian would just have to come out and say it.

"Like our allegiance to the Bruce family?"

Ian wasn't prepared for the man's response. Kelbrue's already-red face turned a shade redder. Could all this anger be because Bruce hadn't informed his allies before attacking Balliol? No, there had to be more to it than that. His was the only clan that pulled support for that one reason.

"Bruce and his intentions to oust the babe be damned."

Ahhh, so that was it. Kelbrue didn't think Bruce should be positioning himself for the throne since the Guardians had publicly declared their support for the Maid of Norway as Scotland's next queen.

Ross himself was one of the Guardians. This was more common ground.

Plant the seed.

"I agree."

The man's surprise was evident. As they rode into the gatehouse, the same one Ian had approached on foot just a week prior, nearly frozen to death, he considered his next words. One week, and he'd found Grey, married, and embroiled himself in the beginnings of what would blossom into an all-out war sooner rather than later.

He said nothing until they reached the stables, where both of them dismounted. Ian looked back. No servants or deer in sight, just Ross and Grey riding behind them.

"Margaret will be Scotland's queen, and Bruce should accept it," he said, and Kelbrue grunted his agreement. "But more importantly, my bollocks are nearly frozen off. Should we go into the hall to warm?"

Kelbrue slapped him on the back. As fathers-in-law went, he

wasn't such a bad one. But before he could follow him inside, Grey pulled him back as Kelbrue walked away with Ross.

"Are you out of your mind?" His frantic whisper reminded him of the many times one of his brothers had said this very thing after he said something they didn't like in front of the cameras. Inevitably they'd back off a few hours or days later, when they realized his strategy made sense. He might not like working in publicity, but he was damn good at it—the only McCaim who was a true chess player when it came to managing people.

"We need him to back Bruce," Grey pressed. "Keep Margaret out of the conversation. She won't be a factor."

As if he didn't know that. Ian rolled his eyes, ensuring his brother's anger. The thought of which, of course, made Ian laugh.

"This is not a game."

Baby brother. No matter what he did.

"That's where you're wrong, Grey. It is very much a game, and I just made the first move. But unlike you, I can see the final one as well."

Grey cursed under his breath.

"It feels like we're right back home," Ian said, not unkindly. He looked into his brother's eyes. "Will you please just trust me?"

His brother sighed, frosted air coming from his mouth. "I always do."

Ian smiled. "Now can we talk about something more important than who may or may not win some battle that changes the course of history forever?"

His brother laughed, his good humor restored. "And what could possibly be more important than that?"

"My wife, Grey. I have a huge problem with Màiri."

Unlike some of his brothers, he wasn't shy about asking for

dating advice or talking about girlfriends. Or in this case, his wife.

"And what problem is that?"

Ian decided to be brutally honest.

"We can't share the same room. It just won't work. We need alternative sleeping arrangements, but I don't want to break any more rules so . . ."

He couldn't even finish over the sound of his brother's laughter. And then he had the gall to actually walk away.

Why exactly had he been so desperate to reunite with his brothers?

13

"He did not touch me."

Grateful Marian had come to escort her to supper, Màiri made that admission just as they were about to leave her bedchamber. Except Marian immediately turned her back around and shut the door behind them.

"Pardon?" she said.

That morn, Màiri had awoken to an empty bed, something she'd expected given her husband was to spend the day hunting with her father. She'd begun to dress on her own when Alana had arrived to assist her. Her dear maid had not remarked on the clean bedding, likely due to the chambermaid who'd accompanied her.

From that moment onward, Màiri had not been alone with Alana or Marian for the remainder of the day. She'd been brought on a tour of Hightower, despite the fact that she'd been there many times, and spent the midday meal with several of Ian's relatives, many of whom she'd not had an opportunity to meet the evening before.

Perhaps it was bold of her to take her new sister-in-law into her confidences so soon, but tomorrow her father and Alana would be leaving, and Marian had been so warm and kind. She desperately needed someone to talk to about her strange situation.

Màiri had been very prepared to dislike Ian. Angry with him for telling her father about the kiss they'd shared, she had blamed him, perhaps too much, for their predicament. Despite her resentment—maybe because of the copious amount of wine she'd drunk—she had found herself opening to him the night before. Telling him things she'd never told another soul.

It had come as a relief when he'd told her that he didn't plan to consummate the marriage yet. She'd been comforted by the prospect of an evening that consisted of nothing but discussion. And yet, lying beside him in that bed, she'd found herself hoping . . .

Well, it mattered not.

Marian had asked her about the wedding night, and Màiri had given her an honest answer.

And now the other woman simply stared at her, saying nothing.

"Did you say," Marian asked finally, "he did not touch you? Not so much as a kiss?"

"Aye. 'Tis so." Why did it embarrass her to admit it was so?

"Hmmm." Marian tipped her head up, as if looking at something on the ceiling. Pursing her lips together, she seemed to come to some sort of decision. "Forgive my forwardness, but if you'll allow me to ask an impertinent question?"

She nearly laughed at that. "You speak of forwardness after our discussion last eve in this very chamber?"

If possible, Marian looked even lovelier when she smiled. She really was flawless to gaze upon. Unlike herself.

"The man you spoke with in the back of the hall. He was to have been your husband?"

Surprised by the question, Màiri did not know how to answer precisely. Aye? Nay? A bit of both?

"We had hoped someday to convince our fathers, but our clans are enemies."

"Dern," she said, distractedly. "I know of them. Neighbors. Allies to MacKinnish but not to your clan?"

A story Màiri was sick of telling. "Aye."

"You love him?"

This was an even more difficult question. Of course she loved Ambrose.

The feelings you had at that moment. Have you felt that way for Ambrose?

"He was like a brother to me," she admitted.

"The decision to marry. It was his?"

Màiri thought back to the day he'd first asked the question. It had taken her aback, but she'd quickly become accustomed to the idea. It had sounded comfortable, and she was fond enough of him to like the thought of seeing him every day.

"Aye, 'twas Ambrose who proposed that we marry. And both of our fathers agreed we should not."

"But you feel differently about Ian, do you not?"

Màiri would not deny it.

"I suppose so. I did kiss him on our first meeting." Cursing the heat that climbed up her neck, she avoided Marian's gaze.

"'Tis nothing to be ashamed of, desire. Those who believe 'tis evil claim 'tis from the devil. Or they say a woman's desire must be kept locked away until her husband agrees to free it. Some say women should be contained the same way, protected from themselves. But Grey would never believe such a foolish thing. Nor, I suspect, would Ian. They acknowledge that we should be free to make our own choices. If we feel desire, that is our choice. If we sing or dance, it is as worthy a choice as a man wearing a padded codpiece."

Màiri did laugh at her sister-in-law's mention of the odd new fashion for men, seen more often in the south.

"Come, supper is nearly served. We will speak more on this. There is more to Ian than you suspect."

Somewhat reassured by their conversation, and extremely curious about that last statement, Màiri followed Marian to the hall. As soon as they walked in, she found herself sweeping the space with her eyes, but the men had not yet returned.

Partway through the meal, a movement at the hall's entrance announced the return of the hunting party. Or so she thought at first. But only two men walked into the hall, neither of whom appeared to be a part of the hunting party. One of them took an open seat at a trestle table below them, but the other approached the dais.

She had not seen him in more than two years, but the youngest male MacKinnish had not changed at all. He'd always looked so similar to Ross they could be twins. Although his thick beard and overly large bearing might look frightening to an outsider, Màiri knew him to be kind, perhaps the most so of all the MacKinnish brothers.

Once, in fact, there had been talk of a union between her and Alastair. But of all the MacKinnish men, he spent the most time training with Bruce and did not seem inclined to marry.

"Greetings, Lady Màiri."

The poor man appeared quite confused by her presence.

"Greetings, Alastair," she said. "You are undoubtedly confused."

"Aye, lass. I'll admit to being so."

"Come. Join us, and allow me to explain."

As he navigated his way to the empty chair next to her, Màiri introduced him to Marian.

"You've not yet had the pleasure of meeting Lady Marian of Fenwall?"

He bowed to her before sitting down next to Màiri.

"Nay, we missed each other when Alistair was last at Hightower," Marian said.

"A pleasure to meet you," he said to Marian, turning back to Màiri. "How is your father?"

"Father is well. He's hunting presently with Ross. And my husband. Ian, Grey's brother."

Alastair blinked, looked from her to Marian, and then drank deeply. Having finished with the entire mug, he called the servant back. He looked more than a bit surprised: he was shocked.

"Ian McCaim?"

She nodded, eyeing the stew that had been placed in front of her. She'd not eaten much since arriving, and it smelled delicious.

"You are Ian McCaim's wife?"

"Aye."

"And he is here?"

Marian cut in. "He and the others should be back soon, now that the sun is set. They left on a celebratory hunt this morn."

"Celebratory?"

"Ian and I were married but yesterday," Màiri explained.

Alastair took another long swig of ale.

"Ian is here," he muttered to himself.

"Aye," Marian said. "As is Greyson. Do you know something more of . . ." She licked her lips nervously. How had Màiri not noticed it before? Something was amiss. Marian and Alastair looked at each other as if they shared a secret. But how was that possible when they had never met? ". . . of his family?"

Alastair took a long drink and placed a second empty mug on the table in front of him.

"Aye, lass. I've plenty to tell them."

Màiri's chest tightened as she listened to their exchange. It was not their words that sounded off, precisely, but the fact that these two, who had never met, seemed to share a common knowledge. They knew something she did not. Perhaps the very thing Marian had alluded to in her chamber.

"She doesn't know?" Alastair asked.

That broke her reverie. They were both staring at her.

"Nay. She met Ian just a sennight ago. The wedding was a quick one."

"Quick? I should say. What could have necessitated . . ." His words trailed away, and the look on Alastair's face indicated he'd come to the wrong conclusion.

"I was not compromised in the way you are thinking."

More importantly, what precisely was happening here?

"If they're married"—he spoke to Marian again—"she must be told."

She was quickly becoming more angry than curious. They spoke around her, about her, as if she were not sitting beside them. What could possibly be so surprising or upsetting? Was this about another woman? Màiri tried to breathe normally.

"'Tis not what you are thinking," Marian rushed to explain, "but we cannot discuss this here. And 'tis for Ian to tell you." She exchanged a glance with Alastair, as if seeking his help, but he frowned in disapproval.

"I know not why Ian kept it from you, my lady. But as his wife, 'tis imperative you know. Especially now." Turning toward Marian, he said, "There's much I need to tell you. To tell the others."

"What must I know?" Màiri asked. She'd raised her voice a little louder than she should have, perhaps, but the worst sorts of scenarios were flitting through her mind. Where she'd been hungry before, now Màiri's stomach roiled with the possibilities.

"Do not scream, Lady Màiri," Alastair said.

Scream? It had hardly been a scream, but she *wanted* to scream. The not knowing was driving her mad.

"You cannot tell her now," Marian insisted. "Not in front of all. Not before Ian has a chance to explain."

Alastair ignored her, but he did acknowledge Marian's

words. "I have known Lady Màiri my whole life. Her father is a friend, an ally. Why her husband chose not to tell her, I cannot say. But she will learn of it before long."

And although Màiri had been anxious to know what they were talking about, she felt a sudden rush of foreboding.

I don't want to know. I don't want to know.

Alastair leaned toward her and whispered, "Your husband is from the future."

14

IAN THOUGHT he'd run the gamut of tough treatment from the press. Although they mostly stayed away from McCaim Shipping, sometimes there was a dispute with the river pilots, business dealings with a country with iffy policies, or a controversy within the McCaim family. There'd been plenty of those in the past five years.

Enough that he knew what to do when ambushed by the press.

But nothing could have prepared Ian for the eruption the moment he walked into the laird's solar. Although Ian had not yet met his grandfather, who was visiting a neighboring clan with a contingent of men, supposedly his solar chamber was the preferred meeting place for matters of importance within the clan. Seconds after they entered the hall after returning from the hunt, Ian, Grey, and Ross had been pulled aside by Hightower's steward. While the others remained in the hall, Ross had made their apologies and then led them upstairs.

Cursing most of the way—he apparently took issue with the news that his brother Alastair was behind their lack of a meal—

Ross had navigated them up a winding set of stairs and through more corridors than Ian could hope to remember. He tended to agree with his uncle's colorful mutterings. He had been looking forward to a hot meal, a hot bath, and seeing his wife.

That last bit was hard to admit.

But if he were being honest with himself, and Ian was nothing if not honest, Màiri had been on his mind all day. In between asking his uncles covert questions about his mother and stalking the unsuspecting red deer, he'd thought about her. Wondered if she was okay. Part of him had even wanted to tell her about all of the new things he was learning about his mother. Growing up, he and his brother had always assumed she was just a woman borderline obsessed with her Scottish heritage. Now he understood her obsession with King Arthur—whom her brothers loved too—her preference for boar and venison over more common fare, and her insistence that all of her children learn horseback riding.

They'd finally reached the room, after what seemed like hours of weaving through the halls, and Ross was the one to open the door.

Ian wasn't sure what he'd expected, but Màiri and Marian glaring at him as if he'd just stolen a puppy wasn't it.

Everyone began talking at once, until Ross's voice could be heard over all others. "Welcome home, Alastair."

His uncle was looking at him. "Ian, I presume?"

"The very same."

"I am your uncle Alastair."

Which wasn't their cover story but the truth. Ian's eyes flew to his wife's.

She knew.

Fuck.

"You told her?" Grey asked before he could.

"And you must be Greyson?"

"I am."

"Aye, I told her. She had a right to know."

Grey jumped in to defend him, but Ian cut him off. He did not need defending. Although he was annoyed Alastair had jumped the gun, as it were, he agreed with the sentiment.

"She did," he agreed, watching Màiri from the corner of his eye. Did she believe it? "But we thought it was too soon. With a shotgun wedding..."

"A quick wedding," Grey muttered.

"A quick wedding," he agreed, "which was actually just yesterday, I figured a few days to get to know me first might be in order."

Alastair made the same grunting sound as his other uncles. Who would've thought a grunt could be so expressive?

"They just met a sennight ago," Colban said, sounding good and pissed. "No one but you thought she was ready."

His youngest uncle apparently disagreed. "No one is ever ready to learn such a thing. But she'd know of it soon enough. Rhys and Reikart make their way here now."

Ian looked at Greyson then. His brother's expression gutted him. For a moment, every other person in the room faded away but Alastair and Grey. What the hell was happening?

He glanced briefly at Màiri. She was looking more confused than hostile. Understandably so.

"Maybe we should all sit."

"Tell us what's happening." Grey wasn't dicking around. This was the tone he'd inherited from the very woman they discussed. People thought their father had been the tough one in the family, but only if they didn't know Shona McCaim.

Alastair shifted his attention back to him. His uncle didn't appear to be offended by his harsh tone. "They've been looking for you."

"Me? But how do they know—" He apologized to Màiri with

his eyes. The poor woman probably thought they were all batshit crazy. Shifting his attention back to Alastair, he finished. "How do they know I came through?"

"Word has been spreading of the strange-speaking McCaim brothers. After we took back Castle Lochlavine—you'll learn the truth eventually, so I'll apologize now for trying to kill Reikart before I knew who he was—I spent some time with your brothers. There's much to tell, but most importantly, they will be on their way here."

"They're coming." Ian and Grey had been counting on this. Waiting for it. But to hear it confirmed . . .

Was it really possible? All of the McCaim brothers had made it safely back to the same time and would be reunited?

Ian did not want to lose it in front of his mother's family. His wife. But he couldn't keep it together either. Grey's arms were around him before he had a chance to react. Reminded of the day of Rhys's disappearance, when Grey had literally picked him up off the floor, Ian held on tight.

He didn't give a fuck who was watching.

"Thank God. Grey, they're coming."

Ian usually bristled against his status as baby of the family, but not right now. Wiping his wet eyes on his brother's shoulders, he repeated the quasi-prayer again.

Grey was the one who finally pulled away.

Ian moved to wipe the remaining wetness from his cheeks, but then his eyes fell on the mark on Màiri's cheek. She couldn't hide it, so he wouldn't hide his tears either. Screw the whole *men aren't supposed to cry* thing. He was a modern man, wasn't he?

Grey, on the other hand, already looked cool and collected again. It struck him that his brother belonged here more than he did. He would fit right in with their uncles. Which was when a new thought hit him, one that drowned out the conversation between Ross and Alastair.

What if some of his brothers wanted to stay?

Màiri had stood and made her way toward him. Ian didn't ask permission to leave or say anything else. He just took her hand and started walking. He meant to bring her back to their chamber so they could talk privately. She came with him willingly enough and did not comment—not even when they ended up at a side entrance to the hall. So much for his masterful tracking skills.

"Master Ian. How may I serve you?"

He peered around the corner to see the rest of their hunting party sitting at two tables, eating the leftovers from supper. No one had bothered sitting on the dais.

Backing up so the others wouldn't see them, he asked, "A meal and a hot bath in our chamber, if you please?"

With a nod, the boy scurried away when he realized a bath required clothing to be discarded. He really couldn't think straight.

Maybe he should rethink having an assistant. If he was going to toil away at a job he hated for the rest of his life, why resist help? When he got back, he was going to hire one immediately.

And he'd have that chance soon. If his brothers were returning, they were going home. It was hard to believe.

"You have every right to be pissed," he said when they were far enough away from the hall to speak privately. This time, he was pretty sure they were headed in the right direction.

"I felt like a fool," she said bitterly. "When Alastair and Marian spoke at supper, I quickly realized they knew something I did not. I could only imagine the cause."

There was no feeling in the world worse than being left out.

Ian knew it well. Felt it pretty much every time he was with his brothers at work. They loved their roles at McCaim Shipping. He was the freak of the family in that regard.

Not that any of the others knew it.

"I'm sorry."

And he truly was. He made a pretty shitty husband.

They must have been walking pretty slow. When they reached their bedchamber, servants piled in behind them. An army of them.

Two with a wooden tub. Three with buckets of hot water. And two more carrying a tray of food and wine.

Apparently they were having a quasi-party in their chamber. While more buckets were brought in, Màiri's maid showed up and herded her into the adjoining dressing chamber. He couldn't wait any longer. Ian sat and began to eat the spiced stew like his life depended on it.

There was a joke in their family: *don't disturb Ian when he's eating.*

He took food very, very seriously.

By the time he finished the stew and freshly baked bread, the tub was filled, but Màiri was nowhere to be found. Stepping around the stool with soap and the medieval version of a towel —more damn linen—Ian gladly removed his cold, wet clothes and stepped inside.

Heaven. Pure, unadulterated heaven.

And then she walked through the adjoining door. Alana must have left through the other exit, thankfully—he hadn't thought about that before he'd undressed. If the tub was heaven, his wife was one of its angels. But the thoughts that ran through his head just then? Anything but angelic.

In fact, they were just the opposite. Which made him feel like the devil's minion—an accurate description if the images he'd just conjured in his mind were any indication.

If he was going to survive until his family made it to Hightower, he would have to get a grip. But at this moment, the only thing he wanted to grip were his wife's hips. He imagined pulling her down into the tub with him, initiating her into this marriage for real.

"Ian?"

He couldn't really talk at the moment.

"Mmmmm."

"You look like you're in pain."

His laugh sounded devilish even to his own ears.

15

THIS HAD BEEN the strangest day of Màiri's short life.

From confusion to disbelief, from anger to sadness . . . and now this. She'd not been prepared to see Ian unclothed, one muscular leg draped over the side of the wooden tub, hands propped behind his head. He appeared to care for naught at the moment.

That wasn't quite true.

As relaxed as he appeared from a distance, her perception changed as she moved closer and the firelight illuminated his face. His eyes.

Which was when she'd blurted out that ridiculous statement. For as soon as the words left her lips, she realized it was not pain that contorted his face at all.

It was desire.

Her lack of experience might be glaring, but Màiri had seen that expression on Ambrose's face before. Not as intense, but it had been there nonetheless. Once, they'd even discussed it—Ambrose telling her precisely when he'd stopped thinking of her as only a friend but as a potential marriage partner.

At first, she'd been shocked. But the more Màiri had thought on it, the more the idea had grown on her. Ambrose accepted her, mark and all. He was kind. He was someone she'd known her whole life. He also lived close to her father, a fact she had hoped might sway her father to set aside his newfound hatred of Clan Dern. But in the end, it had mattered naught.

Perhaps it was for the best.

She could not help but smile at her husband, despite all of the unbelievable things she'd learned this day.

Or maybe because of them. He really had struggled to fit into this time.

"You laugh at me," she accused. "I did not expect to find you . . . in such a state."

"How did you expect to find me?"

"Clothed," she blurted.

Ian's brows raised. He pulled his leg back into the tub and leaned over it to grab the soap sitting on a stool beside it. His back, as broad and muscular as the rest of him, was fully presented to her.

"Is that so?" Sitting back in the water, he gestured to the stool. "Will you sit? Clearly we have a lot to discuss."

Hesitantly, Màiri moved to the other side of the tub, closer to the fire. As if she needed its heat for warmth. She was sure her cheeks had been inflamed since she stepped inside the bedchamber.

Màiri moved the drying cloth and hiked up her shift. Sitting on the now-empty stool, she averted her eyes from the tub. Ian's laugh told her that he knew precisely what she was doing and why. But of course it didn't work. Her eyes were drawn to his chest. Expansive, hard . . . she very much desired to touch it.

"I'm sorry you had to find out that way."

Her gaze flew back up to his face. His jaw was no longer clean-shaven, and a few days of growth had made him appear older. His serious expression unsettled Màiri. It was unusual for Ian, and she liked it not.

"I was angry," she said. "Before."

"Before?"

"Your brother's embrace. I know we've not known each other for very long, but when it became evident Marian and Alastair knew something I did not, the meal became an uncomfortable one. It was not a pleasant feeling. Fortunately, Alastair thought to tell me what you and Marian did not."

Màiri continued to ignore Ian's hand as it glided across his lovely chest with the soap.

"It's not something you tell a stranger. 'So, by the way, I time-traveled back from the twenty-first century.'"

"But I am your wife."

"And a stranger still."

His hand dipped between his legs. Though she couldn't see through the water thanks to the dim light and film of soap on top, Màiri was surprised by how much she suddenly wanted to.

"Do you believe it?"

She'd been caught looking again.

"Aye. I do."

Ian didn't hide his surprise. "You believe I'm from the future?"

"Aye," she repeated. "'Tis not so difficult to imagine. I've always known there are forces beyond what my eyes can see. I believe in many things I cannot touch or feel."

Ian groaned.

She would hear the sound again.

"I take it Marian showed you Grey's cell phone?"

A perceptive man, her husband.

"Aye, she did. Though 'twas 'dead,' as she called it, 'tis not from this time. And so much else suddenly made sense. Your strange manner of speech. The fact that Laird MacKinnish suddenly has a sister-in-law none knew of before. Your . . .

familiarity with me, which Marian says is more customary in your time."

"Kind of. I still don't usually make a habit of kissing women at first sight."

"'Tis extraordinary, really. And I am glad your family will be reunited."

That he had let such vulnerability be witnessed by his uncles, by her, was further proof that he and his brother came from a very different place. She'd heard the Fae were capable of wonders. But to create a traveling chant that could transport people through time?

It was remarkable. Miraculous. Beyond anything she'd ever thought possible.

Ian glided the soap against his neck and back. Frowning, knowing she was begging to be hurt, Màiri made the offer anyway.

"Shall I do that for you?"

His hand froze.

"'Tis customary in my time for a lady to bathe her guests," she explained, lest he misunderstand.

"But I'm not your guest. Not exactly."

She should not have offered.

Ian slowly reached out his hand, the musk-scented soap nestled inside of it.

Moving the stool closer, Màiri took it from his strong fingers, immediately reminded of the kiss they had shared. Of how he'd not hesitated, his lips both soft and demanding. Of how he'd reached that same hand up and cupped her breast.

"Move this way." She took the soap from him, then gently pushed him forward and began to wash his back. Pushing aside wisps of hair from his neck, she pretended Ian was a guest at Kinross.

But the pretense was not convincing. No guest at Kinross had looked like this, felt like this . . . Then his hand snaked up and grasped her wrist, the soap dropping from her slick fingers. He shifted in the tub so she was no longer completely behind him but facing him instead. The iron grip on her wrist did not lessen one bit.

"I'm not from your time, Màiri."

She understood what he was saying. It was partly what had upset her so this evening. Once the pieces had fallen into place, she'd realized why he had not touched her the night before. Why he had not made her his wife in truth.

This was the same man whose honor had prevented him from lying to her father. He'd not take her virginity, chance giving her a babe, and then leave.

And it was evident that was just what he and his family intended.

To go home.

"I know it well," she said softly, regret dripping from her voice.

"When my family arrives, we will use the cross I brought with me to go back to my time. I won't take something as precious as your virginity. Or leave knowing you could be pregnant, even if we take . . . precautions."

He said nothing she had not thought of already, and yet the words still stung. A foolish part of her had hoped . . .

But of course he did not want her to come with him, wife or no.

She was a stranger.

He had said as much more than once.

"You woke this part of me," she accused.

His hand still gripped her wrist. His chest, dripping with water and heaving up and down, betrayed his calm expression. She affected him too—at least she knew that.

"And I regret that."

Màiri pulled her wrist free. At least she fully understood their position.

"And I regret you will have to wash your own back."

In fact, she regretted more than that, but it was a start. He called her name, but Màiri did not look back. Few nobles slept in the same bed, anyway, as few of them married for love. The well-appointed dressing room would be her bedchamber this eve, and every one after it until Ian left.

16

"May I speak with you, Laird?"

He was learning.

Ian may not be book smart like Rhys and Grey, but he knew people. And he felt he'd gotten to know Laird Kelbrue fairly well.

To a fault, the chief was stubborn. Maybe more so than Ian's own father. He'd finally learned about the slight that had caused this entire mess with Bruce, and it wasn't the latter's attack on John Balliol. Sure, that had ruffled Kelbrue's feathers, but he'd said something else in the hunt that Ian had remembered last night as he lay awake thinking of his wife.

Kelbrue had called the grandfather of the man Ian knew would one day rule Scotland a Sassenach lover. At least, that had been his meaning. Kelbrue saw Bruce's diplomacy with King Edward and the English border lords, a diplomacy the grandson would continue well into the War of Independence, as inherently negative. Even history treated Robert the Bruce's initial alliance with King Edward as a kick to the balls. Why wouldn't a man like Kelbrue feel the same way?

The laird had been about to leave the hall, but Màiri had made an appearance to say goodbye to her maid. If Alana weren't leaving, he had no doubt his wife would still be avoiding him. Which, after he'd cooled off, Ian had realized might be the best thing for them.

Because he sure as hell couldn't trust himself to keep his hands off her otherwise.

His father-in-law's response wrested him from his thoughts.

"'Tis a good man, my daughter's husband," Kelbrue boasted to Alastair, who stood beside him. His uncle shot him a look that indicated he did not share the man's opinion. He thought Ian should have told Màiri sooner. It was a ridiculous expectation given the timeline of their relationship, but the last thing he wanted was to get in a pissing match with his mother's youngest brother. So he extended an olive branch.

"I come from good stock," he said, looking directly at his uncle.

The man only grunted. But Ian was determined to get on his good side. He was nothing if not persistent.

"This way, if you would."

Kelbrue followed him to the alcove he'd scouted out for their conversation while Alastair stayed behind. Although it was cold, which was true of pretty much every room in the castle with the exception of the bedchambers, the kitchen, and sometimes the hall, if there were enough people, it was at least fairly private. He gestured for Màiri's father to sit on the cushioned, carved-out wall seat.

"I trust you enjoyed your time at Hightower?" he said as he sat opposite him.

Kelbrue wasn't a man to enjoy pleasantries, so he wasn't overly surprised by the man's response. "As much as one can at the surprise wedding for his only daughter."

Fair enough.

"On my"—he almost said mother's honor—"honor as a member of Clan MacKinnish, Lady Màiri will be well taken care of, Laird. I vow it."

The surest way to get someone to your side? Tell them the truth. Ian didn't feel great about abandoning her, but it was the noblest thing he could do after he'd hijacked her life. Màiri would be home before long, with her father. Together, they could agree on a more suitable husband.

Or maybe the laird would finally let her marry Ambrose.

A man she doesn't love.

Ian pushed the thought to the side. Ambrose, at least, loved her. That much was evident. And from what he'd gathered the last two days, aside from the epic war between Dern and Kelbrue, no one has anything bad to say about Ambrose, his family, or his clan.

Ian shrugged off an image of the two of them together. He wasn't allowed to care.

"I have just one favor to ask in return."

Ian had thought long and hard about this. Grey would kill him. Likely Rhys and Reikart would too. How many times had they begged him not to rock the boat, to leave the planning to them?

Grey and Ross had urged him to butter up Kelbrue without giving him any information, but they were wrong. Kelbrue wasn't the type to make a decision that way. A man with iron-clad convictions did not change his mind because others asked it of him. He would do what he thought was right. He could not know the Maid of Norway would never be queen, but that knowledge should help to change his mind about Bruce.

His approach was better. It might actually work.

"You disavowed your alliance with the Bruce."

From his angry grunt, Laird Kelbrue clearly didn't like this new topic. Although they'd had a friendly chat about the Maid last night, they'd circled away from it.

"But when it comes time, when Màiri shares what she's learned about our family, I ask that you reconsider. Not only for your clan, but for Scotland."

"Never," Kelbrue blustered. "If Bruce wants allies, then he should be honest with them."

It was as if he missed all of Ian's speech except the name *Bruce*.

"Laird, I agree with you. There's no greater dishonor than lying to those who've placed their trust in you. But you've entrusted me to do what is best for the person who is most precious to you. Your daughter. Please just consider my words."

Kelbrue frowned. "What does Màiri know that I do not?"

So he *had* heard him.

"If I could tell you now, I would. But please believe me, someday you will think back on this conversation. Bruce's son, his grandson . . . give them a chance."

His partial admission would probably make the laird leery of him again. But Grey had given him a job, and he'd do it, to the best of his ability. The only shot they had at swaying a man as stubborn as Kelbrue was the truth. When Màiri went back home, Kelbrue would remember this conversation, and perhaps he'd be more inclined to listen once he knew Ian's advice offered the perspective of seven hundred years of history.

It was the best he could do.

"I cannot trust Bruce. But you—" the laird lifted his chin, "—you could have remained silent that day in my hall. I will remember your words. But I cannot vow to abide them."

Kelbrue stood, making it clear he was done with the conversation. But he'd listened, which was more than Ian could have hoped for. Reaching out his hand, he matched his father-in-law's tight grip, more determined than ever to do right by this man's daughter.

But it wouldn't be an easy task, a fact that became ever clearer when he tried to find her after her family left. She was avoiding him. He understood why, but he couldn't see any way out. Ian would not screw around with her and then disappear as quickly as an order of beignets at his team's meetings.

"What the hell did you do to her?" Grey asked.

Ian had just come back from a walk around Hightower. He'd gone looking for his wife and hadn't found her. Along the way, he'd paid attention to every building, every chamber. Someday he would tell his future nieces or nephews about this adventure. And, not for the first time, he wished his parents had told them the truth sooner. He would have taken more of an interest in his heritage had he known this was his mother's world.

"Did you see the chapel? It puts the murals in St. Louis to shame."

His brother didn't appear impressed. Falling in beside him, Grey continued to scowl until Ian finally asked, "Are you talking about Màiri?"

If Grey thought Ian was headed straight for the hall, he was in for a surprise. Unlike his brother, Ian enjoyed wandering aimlessly. Especially these castle corridors. He did it a lot back home, driving his brothers, especially Reikart, insane.

This would be fun.

"No, dipshit. Your other wife."

"So you're Dr. Ruth now?"

He turned down a poorly lit corridor, amazed at how dark certain parts of the castle were compared with others where arrow slits faced the sun. "Can you imagine being a candle-maker? They must be richer than the king."

"Ian."

He hated that tone.

Stopping, he crossed his arms.

"I didn't do anything. That's the point. I've kept my hands off her, and it's not so fucking easy, I might add. Instead of a 'Good job, Ian. Way to not get your wife pregnant and pull the ultimate absent-father disappearing act,' you're upset for God knows why? I'll have you know I took care of your little *Kelbrue's future son saves Bruce's ass at Bannockburn* problem."

That had Grey's attention.

"Only you would call Scotland's War of Independence a little problem," his brother said, leaning against a wall inches away from their only light source in the dimly lit corridor.

"I got to know him a bit yesterday, and I'm telling you there's no way in hell he was going to be sweet-talked into it."

Grey looked at him like, *So how, exactly, did you take care of it?*

"When we go back, we do it in front of Màiri. It's one thing to believe and another to actually see it happen."

"And?"

"Her father likes me. No surprise there," he muttered, though Grey didn't comment on that one. "I told him there's a special reason he should support the Bruce. I told him I couldn't explain yet, but that Màiri will come to him at some point in the future. I urged him to remember our conversation when she does—and to give real consideration to accepting Bruce as an ally again."

Greyson lost it, which was pretty much what he'd expected.

"Seriously? Your answer is for Màiri to tell her father the truth? He'll more likely think we, and Clan MacKinnish by extension, are fucking mad. Why not just disappear in front of father and daughter both if you're going to tell him we're time travelers?"

He'd considered that. But he suspected his brother wouldn't like the reason he'd thrown out the idea. Better to avoid the topic if possible.

"Ian, I swear . . ."

"He was never going to do it otherwise. You're a genius, Grey. You and Rhys both. And Reikart has balls of steel. And yes, I'm just the baby brother."

"I never said that."

"But I can read people. And I'm telling you, there was no other option. He likes me. And trusts me. When Màiri tells him what happened, he will listen to her. I swear it."

"How'd he react to your crazy talk?"

Grey was coming around to the idea. Maybe.

"He seemed receptive, mostly because I'm the crazy fucker who got himself hitched because he can't tell a lie. So yes, he said he would consider it. And I believe him. You want Kelbrue to fight with Bruce? It's done."

"If we can actually get back. And if he believes it. And if he keeps his word."

His word. Kind of. But Ian wouldn't elaborate on Kelbrue's exact wording. He was going with his gut on this one.

"We will."

Grey smiled finally. But his smile was strained.

"What is it?" Something was wrong.

"You left before Alastair could finish his story. And then you were with Màiri . . ."

"Grey," he warned.

"Mom has gone home."

He stared, openmouthed.

"They got the cross back. When word of another brother, you, reached Lochlavine . . . you were the last of us. Rhys and Reik knew you'd have the cross."

No. Mom, no. I was so close to seeing her.

"They sent her back to be with Dad."

Ian could see his brother's lips moving, but he couldn't hear him. Mom was no longer in Scotland. She'd gone back. He would not see her when Rhys and Reik arrived.

"Ian, do you hear me? When they get here, we'll all go back. We'll all be together."

He nodded, pretending to be okay.

"It'll all be fine. And with Kelbrue, I suppose it's as good as we can manage. If Ross couldn't convince him . . ."

"No one could."

As Grey thought about his reassurance, Ian held himself back. He was supposed to care about this war, for Mom's sake. But all he could think about was how he wouldn't be reunited with her. "So it's done?"

"Yep."

"OK, then."

His chest swelled with pride. It felt good to have finally done something right after the whole unexpected wedding hiccup. "OK, then."

He started walking again. Grey followed.

"You never answered me," his brother said, because of course he couldn't have let it lie. "Why not just let him witness the whole thing himself? Why rely on Màiri to convince him?"

Ian stared straight ahead, not wanting to see Grey's expression.

"He's kind of a religious man."

"And?"

He swallowed.

"And. There's a possibility—remote I think, but still a possibility . . ." Ian cleared his throat, delaying his answer.

"He might insist she stay with you," Grey guessed.

However slight that possibility might be, it was still there.

"And that would be so awful because . . . ?"

Ian thought of Màiri's hand on his back the night before. He'd been hard as a rock. But lust wasn't love. They hardly knew each other. He barely had his own life together back home.

"Because . . ."

Say it. Because I don't know what I want. Here. Home. I don't have it together like the rest of you. I hate my job. I love you guys and want to be a part of the family, but Monday mornings suck. The press sucks.

Public relations isn't my thing and never will be. And Màiri deserves more. She deserves someone like Ambrose who worships the ground she walks on. Or like you or Rhys, who have your shit together.

But this was the one thing Ian was used to lying about.

"Because a wife would cramp my style."

17

MÀIRI WALKED toward Marian's dressing chamber. She'd been at Hightower for a sennight now, and each day unfolded much the same way. Wake in the chamber adjoining her husband's, dress with the assistance of her new maid, and break her fast with Marian.

The men rose early, training each day despite the weather. It was much the same at Kinross, especially in the winter months. By the midday meal, the men would come indoors to prepare for the largest meal of the day. And like back home, after more training or hunting or hawking, Hightower's minstrel would treat them to songs well into the darkened hours, when the castle would prepare for another night's rest.

It hurt to see glimpses of Ian—even more so because she saw the desire in his eyes on the rare occasions when he looked at her—but she was grateful for Marian. Their talk about the future was entertaining. She enjoyed learning more about it, and yet, she couldn't help but wish the information had come from Ian. Learning about his mother's fate from Marian, and not Ian, told her all she needed to know of the state of their marriage.

The hours stretched out too long, with little to occupy them. While Marian relished freedoms she'd not enjoyed at Fenwall, Màiri found her lack of duties disconcerting. If not for the possibility of starting a war between their clans, she might have returned home now rather than later.

But such an action would create a rift between her father and Clan MacKinnish, and his stubbornness had already cost their clan too many friends. Besides, she knew from both Ian and Marian what the future held, including her future brother's role in Bruce's army. She didn't wish to change the future for the worse. When the time came, it would be her role to convince her father to do what was needed.

And so she bided her time, treating her stay in Hightower as a bridge between her old life and a new one with Ambrose. Because when the time came for her to marry again, she'd not allow her father to sway her. Marrying Ambrose would be good for their clans. He was handsome and kind, and she had no doubt he would make a good husband. A much better one than Ian, surely.

At least he would touch her.

No matter that Marian had told her it was madness to marry a man she did not love, that she should instead try to talk to Ian, work things out. Marian's husband intended to take her with him, come what may. She did not understand.

Shaking her head, she knocked on the door of Marian's chamber. The door was opened a moment later.

But not by Marian.

"Pardon," she said to Greyson, not having expected him. "I did not realize . . ."

Marian appeared behind him, her cheeks rosy with excitement. "'Tis snowing, quite violently. The men are not training today."

"Can I escort you to break your fast in the hall?" Greyson stepped into the corridor, waiting for his wife to join them.

"I will be but a moment," Marian called out to them.

"Of course."

Màiri had spoken to Ian's brother at supper each evening. But this was the first time she had found herself alone with the man. Although they bore a resemblance to one another, Ian's hair was darker and longer than his brother's, and his countenance was much less serious.

It did not take her long to realize Ian looked to Greyson for approval. When she'd broached the topic with Marian, her friend had laughed. She thought Grey felt much the same way about their oldest brother, Rhys.

"Marian says you are adjusting well to Hightower?"

He asked as if knowing it were only partly true.

"Aye, 'tis much the same as my own home. As its closest neighbor, I've been here many times before."

Realizing she'd turned to present her "good" cheek to him, Màiri forced herself to stand still. Alana had gently pointed out the habit when she was younger, and she'd stopped doing it. Mostly. But sometimes she still caught herself attempting to hide that which could not be hidden.

"I have to say, it's remarkable how easily you've accepted us. And our position."

Màiri had become accustomed to speaking this way. The only time they talked freely about Ian and Greyson's past, or rather future, was inside a closed chamber. Otherwise, there was too great of a risk they might be overheard.

"I was taught to believe most things are possible. And I have never known the MacKinnish men to be a fanciful lot. If they believe it . . ." She trailed off, not wanting to say too much out in the open.

"But still, I appreciate the difficult position you're in, my lady."

"Màiri, please."

When Greyson smiled as he did now, his resemblance to Ian was more apparent than ever.

"Has there been any word?" She did not clarify, but he seemed to understand. According to Alastair, Ian and Greyson's family traveled from Castle Lochlavine, so it could be a fortnight or more before they arrived.

"None, unfortunately."

"My apologies."

Marian came rushing out then, closing the wooden door behind her. Her husband grasped her hand the moment she reached his side. Showing affection in front of others must not be as unusual in their time.

And of course, as they walked to the hall, Màiri found herself thinking of her kiss with Ian. As she did when she woke each day, when she sat next to him at the evening meal, when she lay in bed each night . . .

Was he still back in his bedchamber? Or had he already gone to the hall? He might not want her as a wife, but he could have at least escorted her belowstairs.

Her curiosity about his whereabouts only grew when he failed to appear at the meal . . . or afterward. Pretending his absence did not bother her, Màiri went about her morning, and then afternoon, as usual. She resisted asking after him.

The day drew on unbearably, her loneliness made keener by everyone else's lightheartedness. When Greyson and Marian accompanied her back into the hall that evening, conversation and laughter filled her ears as soon as they stepped inside. Her father called this *et cessabit*. Times of peace when training was halted and . . . she looked around the hall, soaking it in. For now, the joy of being alive and fed was foremost on everyone's minds. She wished to take part in it, but . . .

"You're looking thoughtful."

That voice. Màiri hated that the sound of it should affect her so—as if she'd suddenly come alive again.

"Good eve, Ian."

"I've been looking for you."

"I've just arrived," she said stiffly, "escorted by Greyson and Marian."

He looked every bit a MacKinnish, making the fact that he'd evidently traveled to this time with the help of Fae magic all the more unbelievable. Tartan draped over his broad shoulder, Ian McCaim could easily pass for Ian MacKinnish.

"Will you dine with me tonight?"

She glanced toward the dais, where she'd been headed before Ian had stopped her.

"We've dined together every night," Màiri said, confused.

"Not in the hall."

The vespers bell rang then, a signal for all to move to their seats.

"Come with me."

Curious now, if only because this was the most they'd spoken since her father had left, she followed Ian through the back door leading to the kitchens. But instead of entering them, they turned toward a closed door. Taking a wall torch with him, Ian opened it and led her down the spiral stone staircase.

"Can you see okay?"

Màiri could see well enough, but that didn't mean she understood what was happening.

"You asked that I dine with you, and yet . . ."

He turned a corner, and she followed. Still curious. Mayhap a tad apprehensive.

"Here."

Another door, and Màiri certainly wasn't expecting what was on the other side.

"An undercroft," she murmured.

Not a large one, like in Wentworth Abbey just north of here. But it was vaulted similarly, with fewer pillars but no altars. Instead, this underground chamber appeared to be used for storage. With the exception of one trestle table at its center, lit by candles all around.

And a meal at its center.

"Alastair showed it to me. Apparently it's some sort of custom to bring honored guests down here for private meals. It was used last when Bruce and his son visited Hightower last winter. But with the kitchens just above, it stays relatively warm."

She looked from Ian to the table and sighed at its beauty.

"I wanted to make it up to you somehow. Please, sit."

He pulled the bench out for her on one side. Màiri sat as Ian handed her a goblet full of fine French wine.

"Just because we won't be married for long doesn't mean I want to hurt you. Just the opposite."

Màiri took a sip of wine, grateful for the distraction.

"I feel like sh—I feel awful about how everything went down. If I could give you a dime for every time one of my brothers has said my impetuous nature would get me into trouble . . ."

Her confusion must have been evident, because Ian shook his head as he grabbed his drink. "Sorry. A dime is money. In my time. An expression."

"I take some blame for our situation as well," she admitted. "I find myself married to a man who lived in another time, who will return home to his life. But this is my life, and I've no other time or place to return to. Still, I find myself unsure of how to live it."

"Join the club."

She did not understand his meaning.

"Tell me what you want, Màiri. I'll help you with anything you need."

You.

The thought came unbidden, but the truth of it hit her hard. Her heart raced at the memory of him in that tub. She reached for a piece of bread to cover her embarrassment.

What Màiri had thought she wanted—a life with Ambrose—had been shattered by this man. By the way his presence affected her, by his insightful questions, and by the flutters in her stomach, and other places, every time he was near.

But she could not tell him that.

"Thank you for the offer," she muttered finally, popping a piece of the warm bread into her mouth. Ian refilled her wine, which she'd finished much too quickly, and as they ate their meal, somehow, by the grace of God perhaps, she managed to forget about kisses and tubs and pretend Ian was just like Ambrose.

A friend. Someone she could talk to easily who did not look at her as if she were an oddity to be studied. True to his word, Ian did not seem to care about her mark. Indeed, his gaze never lingered on it, and Màiri even forgot to turn her face away from him.

As she asked him about life in the future, Màiri marveled at Ian's ability to make everything around them, including their strange arrangement, fade away. He spoke to her as if she were the only person in this world, and all she knew was this moment.

"Do you think it will work?"

They'd been speaking of his family, of the brothers' struggles to say the chant correctly.

"I do. Rhys stumbled onto the correct pronunciation first, given his knowledge of Gaelic. Greyson mimics Rhys in all things, so I'm not surprised he got it right too. Reikart is more pragmatic. He recorded it and studied the words as he would a new shipping container acquisition."

"And you?"

"I was lucky enough to have three brothers go through before me. As usual, I just went along for the ride."

Màiri sensed something behind his words, a certain bitterness perhaps. She remembered what he'd told her the night of their wedding, that his brothers treated him as the baby of the family.

Shifting on her bench, Màiri noticed the candles getting low. How long had they been down here?

"As usual," she prodded. "What does that mean?"

Ian stared at her for so long she wondered if he had forgotten the question.

"I wanted to work for the family business my whole life," he finally said. "All four of us were groomed for the roles we'd eventually take, including me. The day I was named chief PR officer, it was supposed to be the crowning achievement of my life."

"But it was not? I recall what you said about your . . . job."

"I'm good at what I do. These past few years have been hell. My mother's disappearance was like a black cloud over the company, over our family . . ."

There was a certain hopelessness in his voice she did not like. Màiri wanted to reach out, to comfort him. But she didn't dare.

"Somehow, we got through it. I did my job, but . . ."

"You do not enjoy it."

He'd told her, aye, but she would have guessed it anyway. It was plain to see.

"No. I hate everything about it, actually. Except for working with my brothers."

"Can you not fill another role?"

Ian frowned. "If your brother decided not to follow in your father's footsteps, could he walk away from being the new laird? Maybe become a blacksmith or something that suits him better?"

The bitterness in his voice was so unlike him, Màiri did not know what to say.

"Nay. He could not do that."

They fell silent. Ian finally stood, and so Màiri did the same.

He gestured for her to walk ahead as he turned to reach for the wall torch. She anticipated him moving in the opposite direction and slammed into him quite ungracefully.

"Pardon—" She pushed against his chest to steady herself.

Ian grasped her hand before she could push him away to separate them. Just like he had that day in the tub.

She froze.

Waiting. Wanting. But knowing she had to pull away.

18

Don't do it.

You didn't spend the last week trying to figure out how to start over with her, to make it right, only to fuck everything up again.

Ian's impulsiveness had gotten him into this mess, and he wasn't going to let it continue to screw with Màiri. Not when he knew he would have to leave her. He let her hand go.

But she didn't move. Instead, his wife looked at him as she had that night in the tub. As she had earlier tonight at dinner. It was the look of a woman who'd never experienced passion—and wanted to start with him. Maybe Ambrose could show her . . .

The hell he would.

Ian wove his hand into the hair just above her neck, pulling her head close. And then he kissed her.

For real this time.

One minute, he was coaxing her tongue to tangle with his own, the next, his hands were everywhere. As Màiri kissed him back, all he could think about was showing her more.

Showing her everything.

Blood pounded through his veins, urging him on. To kiss her

harder. To feel, and let her feel too. He was being reckless. Some part of him knew it, the part that had stayed away from her door at night, despite the hundreds of times his eyes had strayed to it. The part of him that had stopped her from washing him in the tub, that had ignored the desire in her eyes.

But the other part of him . . .

"If you had any idea how bad I want this. Want you. Màiri."

Fuck Ambrose. He would not let that man be the first to bring her pleasure.

Ian spun them toward the closest column, pressing her back against it. And then he kissed her again, more slowly. Taking his time, he ran his tongue across her lower lip, teasing her until the telltale pull of his linen shirt told him she wanted more.

Her gown was too damn confining. But Màiri's neck and chest were exposed to him. He should know—he had been staring at the swell of her breasts all night. Indulging himself now, he trailed a path of kisses from her neck downward. Inching the neckline as low as he was able, he let his lips explore every inch of skin not bound by velvet fabric.

"I did not think . . . ," he heard her whisper as if it were some far-off sound.

Ian lifted his head.

"That I wanted you? Are you kidding me? Màiri, I've never wanted a woman more. If you had any idea of your own power."

He grabbed her hand, something that was becoming a habit with them, and then did the stupidest fucking thing yet. Ian guided it downward onto him, watching Màiri's eyes to be sure he wasn't scaring her. He watched as understanding dawned.

"You did that. Tonight. In the tub. The first time we met. At our wedding. Hell, even just knowing you're in the same room does this to me. It's been damn uncomfortable to be around you, Màiri," he admitted.

"That happens"—she moved her hand just enough to force a groan from him—"to every man?"

"Hell no. Not like this. It would be hard to get much done, walking around with a permanent hard-on. But with you . . ."

He removed his hand. But she didn't.

"'Tis wrong, is it not? To touch you this way? The church says so."

God save him from the Middle Ages.

"There are many things wrong in this world. Your time and mine. But pleasure between two consenting adults, married ones especially? No. I don't believe it's wrong."

Finally, thankfully, Màiri took her hand from him.

"And still, something has stopped you."

That very same hand that had felt him—and how badly he ached to make them man and wife in truth—flew up, and no fucking way was he going to let her cover her cheek. Was Màiri even aware of how often she did it? How often she turned as she spoke, attempting to hide half of herself?

He captured it midway up, pinning it behind her head.

"You are beautiful."

Ian took her second hand, pinning it on the other side of her head.

"Not in spite of it—" he nodded toward her birthmark, "—but because of it."

He leaned forward, kissed that very mark, and then kissed her again on the lips. Pressing into her, Ian stopped thinking. He had one goal now, and he'd not be deterred.

It wasn't the ideal time or place, or even the ideal way to do it. But as he circled his hips against her, plunging his tongue into her mouth with every press of their hips, Ian became more confident it was all he'd need to give her pleasure. For now.

Breathing heavier, pressing harder, Màiri was close. And it was his job to put her over the edge.

"This is just the beginning," he whispered, tightening his grip on her wrists and not relenting as he positioned them as close as possible given the obstruction of the damn gown. "I'm going to make you come once. And then we're going upstairs, where I plan to remove every bit of clothing, and we'll do it again. Properly."

He followed his whispered promise with a kiss just below her ear.

"Let go, my sweet wife. Come for me."

And she did.

19

As Màiri's heartbeat slowly returned to normal, she tried to make sense of what had just happened. She was a virgin still, of course, and yet her entire body had become possessed by something. The devil certainly.

"'Twas not natural," she said as Ian lowered her arms from above her head and stepped back.

"I can assure you, that was very natural."

Màiri's chest rose and fell as she watched Ian grab both of their goblets from the table. By now, all of the candles had burned even lower, the best light coming from the torch he'd brought with him. She took the wine he offered, grateful for the burgundy liquid that made its way down her throat. Màiri had always enjoyed wine, but her father did not believe in excess, so she rarely had more than one gobletful. Two on special occasions.

"That?" Màiri asked as she took the wall torch from its perch.

Coming back toward her, Ian appeared so much calmer than she felt. Màiri's heart, despite having slowed a bit, still beat wildly. Her core continued to clench, a feeling as unfamiliar as the one her husband incited every time he was near.

"That," he repeated, eyes narrowing. "Your first orgasm."

It was not a word Màiri knew. She swallowed.

"I'll be honest, Màiri. I have no idea what people think about sex in your time. But I can venture a guess it's not a typical topic of conversation."

"Nay," she agreed. "'Tis not. The church allows it, between married couples, of course. But it is a sin to enjoy it. And there are very many rules about the days on which such an act is allowed. Most of what I know of it comes from Father Abernethy's sermons."

Ian looked as if he would laugh.

"Rules. Days? Sex ed from the church? No wonder we were forced to marry. It's downright . . ." And then he did laugh, richly and loudly.

"What is it?" she asked, smiling even though she did not understand.

Ian nodded toward the stairwell, and they began to walk.

"I almost said it was downright medieval. A word we use to describe this time."

He lifted the torch and gestured for Màiri to step in front of him, onto the stairs.

"I shouldn't laugh. It's kind of a disparaging term meant to describe something not very advanced."

"Hmm." She thought about that for a moment. "But from what you've told me, your time is much more advanced than mine. So why do you say 'tis disparaging?"

"I'd need more than a week to explain the concept of political correctness."

They emerged near the kitchens.

Ian led the way, and at first she thought he was taking her to the hall. The sharpness of her disappointment surprised her, but then he took a sudden left, and she realized he was bringing her to their bedchamber after all. She'd not come from this direction before.

When Màiri realized what he intended, the calm that she had settled into fled like a Lowlander in battle, as her father might say, replaced by an excitement keener than anything she'd ever known. The silence made her even more nervous as Ian yanked open the door to their chamber. The one she'd avoided these past nights.

It wasn't until Ian replaced the wall torch and closed the door behind him that she noticed the look on his face.

Ian appeared as if he were in pain. But she knew better. And her suspicions were confirmed when she found herself hauled up against him. This kiss was neither gentle nor coaxing. It consumed her—*he* consumed her.

How had Ian even known her kirtle tied at the sides? As his lips claimed hers, the feel of his hands on her waist, the kirtle loosening, gave every indication of what was about to happen. He intended to do as he said and unclothe her. And she was going to let him.

When he pulled away to lift it above her head, Màiri caught her husband's eyes. This was not the hesitant man who'd admitted to hating his job. Nor was it the honest one who'd laid bare their secret in front of her father at Kinross.

The man who lifted her shift, tossing it aside as she stood before him, bare except for a pair of leather boots, was as much a MacKinnish warrior as his uncles. Just younger. And more handsome. The awestruck look on his face only contributed to his appeal.

"You are gorgeous."

It wasn't a word Màiri knew, but she could discern the meaning well enough. And she was inclined to think the same of Ian as he tore off his linen shirt. Not taking the time to undress further, he pulled her into his arms. His hands were everywhere as he backed her toward the bed. When he picked her up and placed her in the center of it, she assumed he would join her. Instead, he positioned himself between her legs. Unsure of what to expect, Màiri moved her hands to cover herself, only to have them pushed back.

"No. You have nothing to be ashamed of, Màiri. Your body is as beautiful as the rest of you, more perfect than you realize."

She'd never felt so exposed.

Likely because she had never been nude except in the company of her maid.

"I love your smile."

The muscles in Ian's arms flexed as he ran his hands from her calves upward.

"You're so fucking perfect. I wish you could see yourself as I see you."

She could almost believe him.

"What happened downstairs was not a proper induction into the club."

Màiri opened her mouth to ask what, precisely, he meant, but only a gasp escaped her lips. Ian had leaned forward to kiss the inside of her leg just above her knee.

It was indescribably delicious, and if she'd felt exposed before, it was nothing to how she felt now.

"I apologize," he murmured, looking up at her as his lips trailed a path upward. "For ignoring those beautiful breasts, for not giving you fair warning. But there's no fucking way I'm going to leave you thinking that's how it should be."

Màiri's heart skipped when he said *leave you*, but she pushed the thought aside.

"You say that word often." She pretended it was completely acceptable to have a man's lips on her inner thigh.

"Fuck?"

Màiri grabbed the coverlet with both hands as Ian continued upward.

"It's an extremely versatile word. Verb, adjective, adverb, noun, interjection."

She finally realized what he intended. The thought of him doing that, of him touching her there with no cloth between them . . .

When Màiri instinctively closed her legs, Ian pressed them back open.

"It also happens to describe, in my time, what I'd dearly love to do with you at the moment."

He was lying down now, and . . .

"To be honest, it's a bit of a crude word for making love. But I find it empowering too. Go on. Say it."

Màiri shook her head as his hands moved toward her core. Ian's thumbs were there and then . . . he kissed her. There! Nay, not kissed precisely. But used his tongue to . . .

"Ian. I do not believe this is allowed."

In fact, she knew it was not. Father Abernethy had said clearly, many times in fact, that any touching between a man and woman should be solely to produce a child. And even she knew she could not get with child from what Ian did to her now.

But Màiri would sooner summon the devil than tell him to stop. Too embarrassed to watch, she laid her head down on the pillow. Nay, she could not do that either. It was impossible to lie still while he moved his lips and tongue against her. Gripping the coverlet even tighter, she finally lifted her head.

And caught his eyes. Ian watched her. She could even feel him smile against her. Almost against her own will, Màiri's hips rose to meet him until a somewhat familiar building of intensity inside her threatened to bubble over.

"Ian," she called. In response, he circled his tongue in such a way that her arse shot up from the bed. Màiri's arms and legs and everything inside of her tensed and squeezed as that same sensation overcame every part of her body.

As her core pulsed, Ian was suddenly over her, his lips now on her breasts. "Say my name again," he coaxed. "Fuck. Go ahead."

She did. Screamed it, in fact. And before he could move away, Màiri grabbed the back of her husband's head and held it there, the effect of what he'd just done to her only now edging away.

When she opened her eyes, surprised to find she'd closed them, Ian was leaning over her. Màiri licked her suddenly dry lips.

"Now that," he said with a smile, "was a proper orgasm. Welcome, officially, to the club."

2 0

"Ian, wake the hell up," Grey whispered frantically. "The laird is back . . ."

One thing Ian had learned about having a castle bedchamber: it was like having the ultimate blackout shades. If it weren't for a strong internal clock, servants would be having to wake him up left and right.

"I so miss waking up to the sound of your voice, Grey," he said, sitting up in bed. The last thing he remembered was waking up in the middle of the night practically clutching his wife to his chest. At some point, she'd rolled over, and he must have put his arm around her without realizing it.

"Is that . . . ?"

Ian put his finger to his lips. Màiri was still sleeping. In her shift, thankfully. Ian had possessed enough sense to retrieve her shift for her before they came to bed. Once he was able to cool his arousal enough to walk again. No way could he have kept his hands off her if she'd slept next to him unclothed.

This whole marriage thing was spiraling out of his control. He'd invited her to stay with him last night, and then he'd held her until she fell asleep. And kept her next to him until his thoughts finally settled enough for him to sleep too. And when he'd woken up beside her?

He'd felt happier than he had in a long, long time.

Ian, to use his favorite word he'd so eloquently taught Màiri the night before, was well and truly fucked.

"Màiri," Ian whispered in response to his brother's question. "Yes. And she's still asleep. What time is it?"

The fire had gone out, and it was pitch black now that Grey had closed the door.

"You missed the morning meal."

"Otherwise known as breakfast."

Silence.

Ian was in no mood for Grey's judgements. He'd forgotten about the potency of medieval wine and had a headache to show for it.

"Get up."

Grey opened the door just enough for him to see his hastily discarded shirt and boots. Putting them on quickly, not wanting to wake Màiri, he grabbed a pinch of mint off the table and chewed it as they left the chamber. What he wouldn't do for proper toothpaste . . .

Grey reached over to fix his hair the way he'd done ever since they were kids. His brother seemed to think it was his personal duty to tame his hair, never mind the fact that he was nearly thirty years old.

And this was exactly why he still lived at home even after all three of his brothers had moved out. His father never once smoothed his hair. Or told him he looked like a cross between a surfer and a NYU dropout. And because Dad needed him.

"Sorry. I didn't know she was in there. I thought you slept in separate chambers."

Why the hell hadn't he taken ibuprofen with him before reciting that chant?

"How do they cure headaches now?"

"Headaches? That's what you're curious about? Headaches? Have you thought about the fact that barbers pull teeth without anesthesia as a remedy for cavities?"

"Jesus. No."

"More importantly, why is Màiri sleeping in your bed?"

Ian only had to distract Grey until they reached the hall. "You said the laird is back? Did you meet him yet?"

Grey gave him a look like, *I know what you're doing.* But strangely, he did not call Ian on it. "Not yet," he said. "We were just finishing the meal when someone said he was spotted in the village. He's probably here by now. Took me a half a day to come fetch you."

Judging by the sweat on Grey's brow, he had obviously already been outside training.

"Why not send someone for me?"

His brother shrugged. "I had to come inside anyway to meet him."

Him being their grandfather. All Ian knew about the man was that he'd been at Forge End in the north, quite some distance from Hightower, at some important meeting of Bruce's allies. Uncle Dermot, his second-in-command, was with him. Apparently they'd be meeting them both.

Ian froze.

"Do we tell them?"

He could tell his brother knew exactly what he meant. From one of the books their dad had procured, they knew their grandfather and uncle would die in the war to come . . . but if they warned them, perhaps that fate could be averted. It might be worth it to try.

Or maybe it would affect the future in a dozen different ways no one wanted.

Greyson shook his head.

"We don't tell them."

"You sure? What if we can prevent it?"

"Mom knows a hell of a lot more about everything than we do. If she wanted to tell them, she could have. But we don't have enough details, so for now, we say nothing. Maybe Mom or Rhys has already said something. They know we're from the future, so at least we won't need to explain that."

Shit.

How was he supposed to look his uncle and grandfather in the eyes, knowing both of them would lose their lives in the fight that was to come? But Grey was right, of course. They couldn't be like, *You will be hanged for aiding Bruce. So maybe go ahead and avoid getting caught.*

"It's a lot to take in."

Grey continued toward the great hall. "No shit. Understatement of the year. Now, about Màiri . . ."

"No, Grey. I can't. Not right now."

"Did you sleep with her?"

Ian loved how his brother listened to him.

"She's still a virgin."

"And you still intend to leave her here?"

"Oh, look at that. Just in time."

They'd turned a corner in the passageway to see two men emerge from the stairwell that led to the ground floor and front door of the keep. There was no doubt as to who the men were.

Even if the laird didn't look like a grey-haired version of his sons, his posture proclaimed him as the leader of this place. The guy next to him had to be Dermot, his red hair a close match for Ian's mother's hair.

Neither man seemed to take notice of them as they made their way to the hall.

The hall was nearly empty—the meal Ian had missed had evidently been cleaned up a long time ago. Perhaps the excitement over the laird's return had ensured no one noticed their absence. Well, no one except for Marian—given that she and Màiri typically breakfasted together in her room these days.

"Is Lady Màiri awake?"

Speak of the devil.

He turned to see his sister-in-law, who was giving him the very same grin his brother had perfected, one that hinted at a secret only the two of them knew.

"He's rubbing off on you."

Grey had gone ahead, following the laird and their uncle into the great hall. He intended to do the same, but Marian pulled him aside.

"When she did not come to my chamber this morn, I made some inquiries."

Ian gave his attention to Marian.

"Did you?"

"Aye. I'd thought Màiri must have eaten in her chamber last eve, but then I learned of your private meal and subsequent disappearance from the after-supper festivities."

If Marian thought listening to a flutist constituted festivities, he could hardly wait until she experienced her first carnival season. Smiling at the thought of her on their company float, the vision was immediately replaced by another.

Unlike Marian, this woman was not pale blonde but dark-haired, although her smile was no less radiant. What would Màiri think of a Mardi Gras parade?

What would she think of New Orleans in general?

"I should not interfere," Marian said in a way that said much while saying little.

Ian agreed but stayed silent.

"But she has none here to protect her."

"She has me."

Marian frowned. "But who will protect her heart from you?"

"Marian," his brother called. "Ian. Come, meet Laird MacKinnish."

They turned to see Greyson standing at the end of the passageway and beckoning them toward the hall. Saved again. He and his sister-in-law joined the small group just inside the hall.

"My wife, Lady Marian of Fenwall," Grey said proudly, making the introductions. "And my brother, Ian."

Apparently no one had warned his grandfather and his uncle that he would be here. Both looked at him as if they'd seen a ghost.

"Ian?"

He was surprised when both of the large, fierce-looking men hugged the crap out of him. He knew by now public displays of affection weren't as common in this time, although his mother had clearly taken to them after making the transition to the twenty-first century. She hadn't gone a day without hugging or kissing them, well into adulthood. It had never bothered him, but he could still remember Reik freaking out one day when their mom reached for his hand in the mall.

He'd been all of eleven or twelve at the time.

Mom hadn't pressed him at the mall, but on the ride home, she'd laid into both of them even though Ian hadn't done a thing. If they were embarrassed to be affectionate toward their mother in public, then they could just get over it.

Make no mistake, these men were not two big teddy bears, hugs excluded. He could see where Ross got his size. Too bad their grandmother wasn't alive. Ian would have loved to meet her too.

"Shona's boys," the laird said, his voice thick.

"Father!" Ross chastised, coming up to them. But his grandfather didn't seem concerned that he might have just blown their cover. Luckily no one seemed to have noticed, and the servants continued clearing the hall.

"Welcome home, Laird," more than one of them muttered as they walked by.

"Ye're strappin' young lads." Their grandfather nodded his chin to Dermot. "Are they not proper MacKinnish boys?"

"Men, Father," Dermot corrected, his brogue a touch less thick than his father's. Dermot, from what Ian understood, spent the most time in England of all of the MacKinnish uncles. Given the political climate, garnering favor from across the border was a worthwhile endeavor, even for Highlanders. Grey seemed disgusted by the idea of "switching sides," as the Bruce family would do many times to preserve themselves, but Ian saw it differently. There was a difference between ass-kissing and diplomacy, but sometimes the line could easily blur. Either way, these nobles were tied more closely to their southern neighbors than they realized.

"Though you are right. Men indeed. And more than a few people will be pleased by this development."

His uncle looked directly at him. Ian got the feeling he was the development.

"Lords," the steward said, coming upon them, "would you like to freshen up as I have a meal brought abovestairs?"

Laird MacKinnish clapped the man on the back, nearly toppling him.

"Very good. We shall meet you all there. The lads here shall join me."

Ian noticed Marian step back out of the corner of his eye.

"You as well, Lady Marian."

She didn't hide her look of surprise.

"Have you word from your father?" the laird asked her.

It was an abrupt change of topic, but Ian understood the direction of his grandfather's thoughts. She was openly surprised at being included in their discussion, and to those who knew her background, it was no secret why. Her father was misogynistic to the extreme.

"I did, Laird. He was less than pleased about the events that transpired."

Namely, the fact that Marian had ditched her equally misogynistic intended for Greyson. Too bad, so sad for the English earl. But from the laird's expression, he clearly didn't give a shit what the Earl of Fenwall thought. Good for him. If everyone wasn't so serious, Ian would have actually laughed out loud.

"I shall send my own message to him as well."

Marian thanked the laird but said it would not be necessary. "I've made my peace with him."

Ian's grandfather nodded with an understanding that went beyond the actual words she'd used. It wouldn't matter because Marian wasn't staying.

So he knew they had the ability to go back home.

Ian really had no clue what else they knew, but he was looking forward to finding out.

"We will meet at sext. There is much to discuss."

His grandfather was just about to walk away when his face lit up. Ian turned to see who he was looking at, and it was none other than his wife.

"Lady Màiri, what are you doing here at Hightower?"

Without so much as a glance at him, Màiri ran to his grandfather as if she'd known the man her whole life. Likely because she had. He embraced her with as much warmth as he would a granddaughter.

For a second, all Ian could think was he'd never seen her hair braided before. She must have woken up when Grey had come for him.

"'Tis a pleasure to see you, Laird."

"I am glad to see you, girl."

Girl? Yeah, not so much.

"Is your father here as well?"

"Nay, Laird. He is not."

An awkward silence fell around them, and the reason was obvious. His grandfather had no idea what had happened between them.

Ian stepped forward.

"Lady Màiri is my wife, sir."

Shit. Wrong title. But he'd gotten the point across. And his grandfather did not appear very pleased to hear it. These MacKinnish men were awfully protective of his wife.

21

Màiri was feeling warmer and warmer, unnaturally so, and it wasn't simply because she sat next to Ian. When she woke, she'd been mortified to realize how long she had slept. Now, as she sat next to Ian in the laird's solar chamber, each moment that passed gave her stomach another strange little twist. At first she thought perhaps she'd had too much wine the evening before, but this felt very different.

That her mother had died from an illness that manifested with only a fever and stomach pain did not help matters. Neither, she suspected, did the discussion that swirled around her.

Alastair and Dermot relayed how they'd helped Ian's brother Rhys and his wife, Maggie, take back Castle Lochlavine. She tried to listen to the tale of Ellen, whom she knew as Lady Shona, and how she'd reunited with her family. How they used the cross to send her back after learning Ian had come through.

Rumors that the lord and lady of Lochlavine had been seen at the Black Heart Inn confirmed what they already knew. Ian's family was on their way to Hightower. Soon, they would arrive to use the cross and return to their time.

"Màiri," Ian whispered. "Are you unwell?"

She'd avoided looking at him, embarrassed and unsure after what had happened between them. But she looked at him now and nodded.

"I believe I may be so."

Her head pounded. Her heart beat rapidly, but it felt much different than it had the night before with Ian. Nay, she did not feel well at all. By now conversation around her had stopped, and everyone was looking at her, which only made her feel more conscious of her illness.

Ian stood.

"No," she said, not wanting to interrupt his reunion with his family. "I'm fine. I simply need to rest a bit."

He looked like he had something to say about that. But before he could react, Marian had grabbed Màiri's arm and was escorting her from the chamber.

"Stay, Ian," she said. "I will take care of her."

He answered, but Màiri didn't hear the words. She was having difficulty breathing, but as they walked, her chest seemed to fill with air a bit easier than it had in the solar. Perhaps it had just been too warm in there.

Màiri took out a kerchief and wiped her forehead with it.

"'Tis quite a bit cooler out here." She caught Marian's expression of concern. "Was it not warm in there?"

Marian gently shook her head. "Nay, I did not believe so. But then, I am always cool."

"As am I." She modified, "Except today."

"We shall return to your chamber. I will find the maid to make you comfortable, and fetch a physician as well."

"No!" Marian looked taken aback, so she quickly amended, "That is to say, I do not believe my condition warrants it."

Marian stopped and cocked her head to look at her.

"There is something more, is there not?"

Her stomach roiling, Màiri wanted to deny it. But as her new friend waited, she actually wanted to tell her. To share what happened with someone other than Alana and Ambrose.

"My father blames the physician for my mother's death. She was ill, aye, but it was only after the man visited her that she worsened."

"What illness took her?" Marian asked gently.

"We do not know. It happened in just a few short days. She complained of stomach pain"—Marian's eyes glistened with understanding—"and then a fever."

"Do you believe the physician was responsible?"

"Nay. And yet . . ."

"You do not care to summon one?"

Màiri shook her head.

They walked the rest of the way in silence. When she and Marian entered the dressing chamber, Màiri paused.

"I will help you undress," Marian offered, and when she did not reply, she said, "Màiri?"

"I do not know where to go. Shall I stay here?"

"Where else? Oh."

Marian made no further comment until Màiri had taken off all but her shift. Lying in the bed, the pillows propped behind her, she finally began to breathe normally again.

"You do not have to tell me if you do not wish it."

In fact, Màiri very much wished it. So she told Marian everything. The dinner, and some of what happened between them afterward.

"Do you know what Grey told me?"

The question was clearly rhetorical, but Màiri shook her head.

"In his time, there is no shame in pleasure between two consenting adults. He encourages me to tell him what I like, and whenever I become embarrassed, he encourages me to say the words. And they do come much easier now."

Despite the pain in her head, Màiri felt a rush of excitement.

"Ian and Father Abernethy have very different ideas about relations between a man and woman."

Marian made a face. "Is this the same Father Abernethy that Alastair has complained of?"

Màiri laughed, feeling much better than she had before. "Aye. He and Alastair have never gotten on very well. In fact, few seem to treat well with the priest, with the exception of my father. After Mother passed away, he became even closer to God. I believe 'tis why he will not admit to his feelings for Alana."

"Your maid?" Marian asked, incredulous.

"Aye. I believe they have loved each other for many years."

"Perhaps her position in your household gives him pause?"

"Nay, I do not believe so. My father is not one to live by others' rules in that way."

"Hmmm."

The women exchanged a glance, Màiri every bit aware of the one thing they had not talked about, the most important thing of all. Ian had made his position clear. He did not want a wife. And based on what Laird MacKinnish had said, he would be leaving very soon.

After a lifetime of stares, Màiri knew the expression Marian wore well. It was one of pity.

"I think I might rest," she said, not very tired but wanting to be alone with her thoughts. She appreciated Marian's support, but there was nothing her temporary sister-in-law could do about her current predicament.

She was falling in love with her husband.

HE WAS ALMOST DISAPPOINTED when the creaking door didn't wake her. Marian had said she was fine, but he'd needed to see for himself. The fact that she was sleeping in the middle of the day didn't bode well for her health. Something was wrong. He tried to tell himself that maybe Màiri was overwhelmed with everything. Hell, he certainly was.

But then he noticed the color of her skin. And the fact that she'd started sweating. Something was off, and given what had happened to her mother, how she had died, Ian knew she was probably scared too.

Ian sat in the chair near her bed and stretched his legs out in front of him, watching her sleep.

As usual, she slept on the side of her birthmark. Màiri had gotten pretty good at hiding it. Had probably been doing so her whole life. Kind of like he'd hidden his distaste for the job he'd been bred for in the company. Sometimes it actually pissed him off that not one of his brothers suspected. They were his brothers, for Christ's sake. Even his father had no clue.

But Mom . . .

She had known. Every time he thought of Rhys and Reik coming here, without her, Ian couldn't help feeling angry at being the only one to not have been reunited with her. But with any luck, when his brothers arrived they could all go home and end this nightmare. And, if they were really lucky, hearing Mom's voice might even help pull Dad back from the brink.

Ian really didn't think it would happen, not when his father was this far gone, but it was a hell of a dream.

Màiri stirred, but didn't wake up.

You could take her with you.

After he'd fucked up royally the night before, not once but multiple times, Ian could admit he felt something for her. A big something, in fact. More than he'd ever felt about a woman before. But he wasn't like Grey and Rhys. Ian didn't have his shit together.

He could move out, get his own place.

But being a husband was a hell of a lot more than owning a house. Money wasn't the problem. *He* was the problem.

Could he really settle down with one woman for the rest of his life? If he took Màiri to New Orleans, he would be solely responsible for her happiness. Was he ready for that?

"Ian?"

His brother.

Ian went to the door, stepping outside.

"You're making a bad habit of fetching me when I don't want to be fetched."

He noticed his brother's outfit then. "Is that"—he poked his chest—"armor?"

"We have to go. Marian will be up any minute to sit with her."

"What the hell?"

Grey didn't pull any punches. "There's been an attack on Clan Dern. Someone set fire to the blacksmith's forge in the village. It's our job as their allies to step up."

"Are they sure the blacksmith didn't start his own fire? Seems like a pretty dangerous job."

His brother didn't answer—he just held the door and waited and, like always, Ian followed him. By the time they made their way to the hall, all hell had broken loose. If this was a call to arms, Ian would gladly be a part of it. The energy here was like nothing he'd ever experienced, even before one of his games.

"This way."

Grey had seen a lot more action than he had in this time, so Ian didn't question his brother—he just followed him out into the courtyard. "Hurry to the armorer."

It looked like everyone else was ready. Dozens of men were mounted, including his uncle and grandfather, all carrying weapons. Not everyone wore a plaid draped around them, but some did. Others, like his brother, wore thick leather, not the kind of armor he associated with medieval knights.

But they weren't in England. This was the Highlands.

Known to locals as the mountains. Even without plated armor, or maybe because of its absence, they looked beyond fierce.

Badasses, for sure.

And for the time being, he was one of them.

"Hurry," the armorer called to him, gesturing him toward the same building he walked into every morning before training. Before long, he looked just like Grey, the only difference being that he was packing a sword rather than Grey's bow and arrow. At least he'd become slightly proficient with it. Although it was much lighter than he'd expected, it was the real deal. No blunted tip here.

Of course, if a trained knight got a hold of him, Ian would be toast. He'd have to rely on speed instead. But strangely, he wasn't afraid. Once mounted, he asked Grey if that was normal.

"No. It's not. Unless you have a death wish."

He denied it. "I'm not Reik."

"Wait until you see some real action. Talk to me then."

But there was no real action to see.

By the time they rode to Dern's village, there was no rival clan waiting for them. Just a bunch of angry men shouting about the cowards who had started a fire and fled.

Ian watched as his grandfather dismounted and walked toward another man, who stood in front of what was apparently the forge. Smoke rose up, the smell more acrid than a garderobe, which was truly saying something. They'd taken only forty or so men with them, but to Ian it seemed like an army.

He marveled at how quickly Clan MacKinnish had come to the aid of their allies.

"Who is that?" he asked Grey, who'd reined his horse up next to him.

"Dunno. Maybe Clan Dern's laird?"

Most likely. He was much younger than their grandfather, but Grey was probably right. Then Ian saw the person standing behind him. "Yeah. That's their laird."

"How do you know?"

Ambrose stared straight at him. "Because that's his son right behind him."

"He's coming this way."

To his credit, Grey dismounted as quickly as Ian did. He stood by his side as the laird's son approached, and then he actually took a step forward. His brothers were nothing if not protective.

"Many thanks for coming to our aid," Ambrose said.

Ian wanted to hate the man. He was certainly a coward for not visiting Màiri before the wedding, after he learned she was engaged. But by all accounts, the man in front of him was honorable and kind. An excellent swordsman, most said.

And Ian had most certainly asked around.

"Of course," Ian responded, waiting for the man's next move.

"Is Màiri well?"

He must have hesitated just long enough for Ambrose to pick up on it.

"What is it?"

Grey started to answer, but Ian cut in. He could fight his own battles—something he'd remind Grey of when this was over.

"She's a bit out of sorts at the moment, but she's resting."

So much for trying to fit in. Apparently *out of sorts* wasn't a medieval phrase. Ambrose wrinkled his nose and lifted his chin.

"Her stomach? And pain here?" Ambrose touched his temple. "Perhaps she was warm?"

How the hell did he know all of that?

Ian's eyes narrowed. "Aye."

Ambrose nodded. "It's happened many times," he said. "She worries about something, aye?"

"Greyson," their grandfather shouted, waving to him. Ian nodded for his brother to go. With a final glare at Ambrose, Grey walked off toward the forge.

"Maybe," Ian said, noncommittally. He didn't like this guy knowing so much about his wife.

He knows her better than you. He's known Màiri his whole life.

"If you please, offer her my well-wishes."

Ian couldn't help his scowl. "Sure."

Ambrose was distracted by something in the vicinity of the forge. They both looked in that direction as the laird of Clan Dern pointed behind the forge.

"What's going on?"

Ambrose looked at him strangely. Ian tried not to roll his eyes. "What, pray tell, is happening?"

That didn't help much. He would have laughed aloud if Ambrose didn't look so concerned, but Ian didn't think it was his lame attempt to talk like a medieval person that was bothering the guy.

"We're attempting to learn more about the source of the fire. It looks like Father believes they may have come from the west."

"How do you know?"

"He's pointing to the ground. There must be footprints leading away from the forge."

The west. He didn't have to be a genius to figure out what the laird of Clan Dern was suggesting. The feud between Dern and Kelbrue was legendary.

"Let's have a look."

They walked down to the forge, the smell of smoke burning Ian's lungs. Luckily they'd put it out before the building next to it had gone up in flames too. That could have been one wicked fire.

"Let's see." Ian made his way past both lairds around the stone building, now without a roof. Sure enough, there were footprints everywhere, which made sense. Someone had put out the fire.

"There."

Ian's gaze followed Ambrose's finger. Sure enough, a set of prints as clear as day led into the woods behind the forge.

"What's west of here?" he asked, already knowing the answer.

"Beyond this forge, nothing but woods. And eventually . . ." Ambrose was clearly reluctant to finish the thought.

"Let me guess. Nothing until Kinross."

Ambrose sighed. "They'll blame it on them. Already are," he admitted.

Ian moved toward the footprints. Too perfect. He walked alongside them into the woods and snow. Ambrose followed.

"When did the fire break out?"

Before Ambrose could answer, he continued, "It happened today, I presume. Not overnight?"

"Aye," he answered, "just before sext."

"Come here."

Ambrose leaned over to look at the spot where Ian had pointed.

"Do you see that spiderweb? Just above the prints?"

It was nearly impossible to see with the snow's glare. Or impossible for someone who hadn't conducted their Eagle Project on tracking. Specifically, tracking humans. He wasn't much of a literature buff, but *The Most Dangerous Game* had always fascinated him. He'd had to fight for the topic: tracking human beings was apparently considered more than a bit strange.

"Nay, I do not . . . oh, aye, I see it now."

"Spiders weave their webs late in the evening." At least, they did in modern times, but Ian had no reason to think spiders' behavior had evolved all that much. "Which means those prints were made yesterday. What's more, whoever made them was walking, not running. Which would be strange behavior for someone attempting to flee a crime scene."

Ambrose blinked, unsure what to make of him.

"Incidentally, whoever made those prints favored their right leg. An injured left one, maybe?"

Ambrose's eyes widened.

"You know who it was?"

Clearly he did. And Ian had a good guess as to whodunnit. "An inside job? Someone wanting to frame Clan Kelbrue maybe?"

"God's wounds . . ."

They really did need better curses around here.

"Who did it?" Ian was so curious he forgot for a second he was talking to Màiri's ex. Or sort of ex. Whatever.

"The blacksmith himself."

"Ha!" He hadn't meant to shout. "Sorry. It's just, I told my brother . . . never mind."

"He came to us nearly two years ago, his left leg injured in an accident."

Two years ago. Undoubtedly there'd been plenty of trouble between Clans Dern and Kelbrue in that time. How much of it had been caused by the blacksmith? But Ambrose and his father could figure the rest of it out. Ian's job here was done.

At least he'd averted a clan war for his temporary father-in-law.

"Well, I wish you luck." With that, he turned to walk away.

"McCaim?"

The name startled him. It was his, of course, but he heard it so rarely here.

"Aye?"

He eyed the laird's son, waiting for the hammer to drop. But it never did. Ambrose met his eyes and held them, and said, "She is the best woman I know. Treat her kindly, and love her as I would have."

Jesus. Was this guy for real?

He was about to say, *Yeah sure*, but he realized Ambrose

really meant it. The guy had a ridiculous name, but he was honestly in love with Màiri.

Could he say the same?

Ian couldn't answer him honestly—he'd be lying if he agreed. He was planning to leave her, not love her. Wasn't he?

"You're a good man," was all he said to her former intended, walking away.

A better one than me.

22

"RIDE WITH ME."

Grey didn't ask why. He just called ahead to Ross, telling him they'd return shortly, and when the others made the final climb to the aptly named Hightower Castle, Ian and his brother turned their mounts.

"Nice work back there," Grey said as they continued to ride, their pace less frantic than it had been earlier.

"Thanks." Ian was surprised by how quickly everything had happened. One minute, he was playing Eagle Scout with Ambrose. The next, his wife's "friend" was talking to his father. All hell had broken loose, and they'd seized the smith, who'd admitted to the whole thing but hadn't explained why he'd done it.

"Why do you think the smith wanted to cause trouble between Dern and Kelbrue?"

Grey shook his head. "Who knows. We thought New Orleans politics were out of control, but even the most corrupt commissioners have nothing on these clans."

"Do you think Màiri's father will reconsider his alliance with Dern?"

"No idea." He cracked a smile. "Maybe when he learns his new BFF was the one to crack the code."

"Pfft. I'll hardly be his favorite person soon."

Neither of them spoke as they climbed a ridge, one Ian knew offered an even more spectacular view than Rhys's balcony back home. He loved people watching through the old wrought iron, listening to jazz streaming up from the streets below.

But this . . .

"Spectacular," Grey said, echoing his thoughts. His brother's horse danced beneath him. Steadying the mare, Grey breathed in the cold air, Ian watching him.

"Will you miss it?"

If Rhys and the others were almost at Hightower, this might be the last time they'd look out from this spot to the valley and rivers stretched out beneath them. Even though it was nearly dusk, there were no lights, no buildings even. Only Hightower in the distance behind them.

"We can come back."

"No way . . ."

"I was thinking on a plane. In the twenty-first century."

"Oh." Ian laughed. "Yeah, that I'll do. But it won't be the same."

"No," Grey agreed. "It won't."

Which reminded him. "Do you think it was hard for Mom, when we visited as a family? It must have been," he said, answering his own question.

"I'm sure we didn't visit Hightower for that reason. Can you imagine what Hightower would be like without Uncle Ross or Clan MacKinnish? A bunch of tourists traipsing through what used to be Mom's home, commenting on her old hairbrush?"

No, he couldn't imagine it at all.

"Will I miss it?" Grey asked. "Yes, I will. I mean, look at that. It's like a postcard."

But it was more than the view, and they both knew it.

"I might toss my cell in the river when we get back."

Grey laughed. "I know what you mean. On the other hand, I wake up in the middle of the night dreaming about birthday cake snowballs."

"You don't even like sweets."

"I do when I can't have them."

Ian shoved the thought of shaved ice covered with condensed milk from his mind. No use dreaming about something you can't have.

"I'll miss it too," he agreed, surprised it was true.

But he wouldn't miss the cold.

"We should get back." And yet, when he attempted to turn to do just that, Grey blocked him from leaving. "You didn't ask me to come here to talk about scenery and snowballs. What's up, Ian?"

Grey was right. But he changed his mind.

"Ian?"

A bird, Ian didn't know what kind, swooped down so close to them his brother flinched.

"You kill a man, more than one actually, but are terrified of one wee bird?" he asked, using his best Scottish accent. Grey seemed to appreciate it. His laugh echoed into the valley, and as long as Ian lived, he'd not forget that sound. Or this moment.

If they got back safe and sound, he wouldn't take even one second of time with his family for granted.

"It's Màiri," Grey guessed once his laughter finally dried up.

Well shit, of course it was Màiri. "Our brothers are embroiled in a plot against a king. They may or may not make it back alive, according to some of what you told me about medieval travel. So yeah, let's worry about that and not my wife."

Grey wouldn't let it go. "That's kind of the problem, isn't it? She's your wife. No getting around it."

"Not for long."

"Jesus," Grey muttered. "You're such a stubborn asshole."

So much for their genuine brother-to-brother moment.

"Clearly you care about her. Give me one good reason not to stay married? Not to take her back to New Orleans?"

He could give Grey more than one, but he'd start with his brother's statement.

"I care about her. Desire the hell out of her. But do I love her? Does she love me?" He couldn't believe he was saying this shit out loud. "It's a big deal, to take someone across seven hundred years. There's no going back on that. And I've known her for exactly two weeks."

"True. But I assume you've thought through the alternative?"

The alternative. Leaving Màiri here, in her own time. Returning home to never see her again, never know what had become of her. Maybe she would marry Ambrose. Maybe not. She could do a lot worse, and now that their clans had a reason to rethink an alliance . . .

"I can't tell you what to do," his brother said after a moment. "Obviously. And I'm no expert either. But we've all seen a pretty crystal clear example of love."

"Meaning?"

"Meaning, look at Dad. He's spent every day since Mom disappeared trying to get her back—researching, making calls, bidding on ancient books, you name it. He never once gave up."

Ian didn't want to think of it. His chest literally burned with guilt and shame for the hell they'd put their father through, not believing him.

"And think about what it must have been like for Mom. She gave us everything after having lost"—he swept his hands in front of him—"all of this. Can you imagine? And it must have been so hard for her not to tell us. I can only assume she did it to protect us."

Ian had thought the same thing as well.

But he couldn't bear to think of his parents right now. He

just couldn't. The thought of his father dying alone in that hospital bed, never having known they'd believed him in the end . . . He angrily wiped away a tear.

"How did you know? With Marian?"

Greyson let out a deep breath. "The thought of giving her over to Duncan . . ." He shook his head. "No way. Wasn't going to happen. I just knew."

I just knew.

That was the problem. Ian didn't just know. He felt like Jon Snow. He knew nothing. About his feelings. About his role in their family. Ian was as lost now as he'd been that day his mother had confronted him in the kitchen.

And that wasn't good enough for Màiri.

She worries about something, aye?

He wasn't sure why Ambrose's question popped into his brain just then. But it had. And he felt like an idiot for not realizing it sooner.

"Anxiety."

"Yeah, you cause it all the time."

Ian made a face at his brother as they left the overlook and approached the castle.

"Stomach problems. Sweating. Trouble breathing. Ambrose said she's had symptoms like that before. He implied it happens more often when she worries."

"Hmmm."

"Think about Reik. Especially just after the accident. Anxiety, Grey. She has anxiety. Sitting in that room with everyone, not knowing what her future holds. I did that to her. Dammit, I'm such an idiot."

"I don't disagree with you there."

"I can fix this."

He raced ahead of his brother. How had it not occurred to him earlier? The way he'd been treating Màiri was causing her to be physically ill. Of course, that wasn't something they could diagnose now, but if she felt better when he got back ...

No more mixed signals. No more uncertainty. No more waiting.

Ian couldn't fix his own situation, but he could help hers.

23

MÀIRI HAD DECIDED to tell Ian how she felt about him.

If his family was almost here, they didn't have much time left. There was no doubt she was falling in love with him, and Màiri would not let him leave without saying so.

She'd dressed with the help of the maid, putting on the finest gown she'd brought from Kinross, and styling her hair so it was piled atop her head. Her mark was in plain sight.

Not wanting to speak with him around the others, she waited for him in their chamber, planning to tell him straight-away. But when he burst through the door not long after, armored and looking very much from her time, he spoke before she could, and what he said left her openmouthed.

"I should never have been so selfish last night. Obviously I desire you Màiri. I have since the very first day we met. But I swear, I never intended to seduce you. That dinner was supposed to be a peace offering. And then . . . things just got out of control. I am so sorry, for all of it. I spoke with Ambrose today, and he's a really good guy. And you're right. He loves you. You deserve a man like that."

She could not believe what she was hearing.

"What are you saying?"

"You shouldn't have to sit here and wait for my family to arrive to begin your life. I won't hold you back. I mean it. If you want to go to Ambrose, we can tell him everything. Or we can go to your father and share the truth with him. Maybe that will make it easier. I don't care who knows or who believes what. Anything you need, Màiri. Tell me, and I'll help."

Her skin prickled everywhere as she listened to him. Her neck and arms, all over her scalp. She had to be dreaming.

She hoped she was dreaming.

"I know what was wrong earlier. At Dern, I talked to Ambrose . . ."

"You . . ." Had she heard correctly? ". . . spoke with Ambrose?"

"I did. And I'll tell you about that later. But he told me this has happened before and asked if you were worried about anything. You're feeling better now, right?" Without waiting for her answer, Ian, as excitable as she'd ever seen him, continued, "It's called anxiety. My brother suffers from it, so badly sometimes he has panic attacks. I mean, we all have it to some degree, but . . . never mind. What's important is that you feel better. And I know what caused it."

"You do?"

Had she really spent the day thinking of him? Thinking of the way he made her feel when they were together? Thinking of how to make him understand she didn't wish to be parted from him?

"I do. It was me."

Màiri struggled to focus on his words.

"I caused it. So I need you to think about this."

As he spoke, Ian unwrapped the plaid that sometimes made her forget he wasn't from her time. Dipping a linen strip into the bowl of water near the bed, he wiped his face.

Please, Ian, no.

His shirt came off next. She hardly heard his words as he cleaned himself for supper.

"You shouldn't have to sit here and wait with the rest of us. Think about it tonight and let me know what you want to do. Tomorrow, I'll take you anywhere. Talk to anyone. Explain whatever you need me to explain to make this right."

Ian was so carried away by the thought of this supposed solution that he somehow forgot she was standing there, watching him. He stripped down completely, reaching for fresh clothing. In doing so, Màiri had a clear view of his backside. All of it.

And then he turned.

Saw her watching.

"Ah shit."

Right before her eyes, it grew. Màiri's eyes widened as she watched, never having seen the frontside of a man before. She'd washed honored guests, but they had, of course, been covered with soapy water. And another maid had always been present on such occasions.

Perhaps it was best this way. The thought of him, of that, inside her was an alarming one. Surely Marian had been wrong. That hurt only a bit the first time? Would she have lied? Surely not, but how was that possible?

He covered himself, but not quickly enough. Even when he was fully dressed she could still see the bulge beneath his braies. Màiri knew now, she understood. And could not unsee the vision of her husband naked before her, hard with longing.

"Màiri?"

She looked up.

"We should probably not be in a room alone."

Màiri opened her mouth, but no sound came out. She resisted the sudden urge to grab the closest item to her and toss it at her husband. He thought to make things right between them by escorting her, a married woman, to Ambrose Dern?

And explaining that he was from the future, so she was free to marry another? Did this man truly have no sense?

She did the only thing possible. Màiri turned and walked back into the attached dressing chamber. From there, she began to throw every item she'd taken from her bags back inside of them.

Nay, she could not go home this eve. It was already dark. But she was having difficulty thinking clearly.

Leaving the chamber just as Ian entered it through their shared door, Màiri hastened away before he could follow. He wore no boots. Would he come after her in bare feet? Aye, the man was likely to do anything he pleased.

She couldn't go to the hall. Not like this. Not yet. Instead, she ran to the only person she could possibly talk to. Perhaps Marian had not gone yet to supper. By the time she reached her door, Màiri was no longer surprised by his behavior. Or saddened.

She was angry. As angry as her father when he'd drained the loch. A part of her thought to turn back around and tell Ian every thought that ran through her mind. But to what end? Did she really want to convince a man so desperate to get rid of her to care for her as she cared for him?

Her hand paused just before she knocked.

Màiri thought of Ambrose.

So this was how he felt. While she adored him, cared for him like one of her own family members, his feelings were different from hers. The horrible feelings of rage and anger and sadness and loss coursing through her were the downside of romantic love. She loved Ian, but he did not feel the same. She could not go to Ambrose knowing he might feel this way for her and she loved him like a brother in return.

She could never marry him.

It would be cruel to do so knowing what she did now.

"Màiri!"

The door opened before she knocked. Màiri had not intended to cry, but the moment she saw Marian's face, she crumpled. Rage turned to despair as the tears began to flow. Her friend, nay, her sister-in-law, ran to her, held Màiri in her arms.

"He never cared," she sobbed as Marian led them into her chamber.

"Ian never cared for you?" Marian's voice seemed a thousand yards away.

"Nay . . . aye . . . but I meant . . ." Her thoughts were erratic. "He truly never cared that my face is marred."

"Marred?" Marian scolded. "Oh, Màiri, 'tis a mark, is all. We all have one. Some on our faces. Others etched much deeper, on our very souls. But I've not met one person in my life who was not marred in some way. 'Tis what makes you, you."

Alana had always said much the same.

The door clicked shut.

Màiri moved away. "Was that . . . ?"

"Grey just left, aye. Do not concern yourself about him. I shall have a meal brought to us."

"No." She shook her head. "No, you go to supper."

"Absolutely not."

Màiri startled at the strange remark.

"Sorry. Grey says it often. He is influencing me just as we are him."

Màiri hardly heard her words. Her shoulders sagged. "We are done. Ian and I."

"Shut up!"

"Pardon?"

"I am sorry. It is just another phrase he taught me. 'Tis quite versatile, in fact. The way I used it just now, it means something akin to *you do not say*. But there are other meanings too. Such as *stop talking*, which I'd not have you do. 'Twas just the first phrase that came to mind."

She loved when Marian's enthusiasm got away with her, or

when she was so eager to comfort someone she spoke too quickly, letting her point escape her somewhere along the way. Màiri would miss her terribly.

"Ian taught me a word as well," she admitted. "Though I do not believe I can say it to you now."

"Did he?" Marian leaned forward. "Tell me. Go ahead. Say it."

She thought of Ian. Of his rejection. And of what they'd been doing when he had taught her this very word.

"Go on."

Màiri took a deep breath and let it out. "Fuck."

Both women burst into laughter, Màiri testing the word again. Ian had said she could use it in many different ways.

"Fuck him," she tried.

Ian was right. It was indeed a powerful word. Màiri already felt a bit better.

24

"WHAT THE HELL do you mean, gone?"

Perhaps it wasn't the kindest way to speak to his sister-in-law, but it wasn't every day a man's sister-in-law informed him that his wife had left him.

Of course, he had no one to blame but himself.

All morning, Ian had felt unsettled. Màiri hadn't come down to the meal the night before, not that he was surprised. Grey had tried to talk to him about it, more than once, but he'd carefully avoided his brother by sitting as far from him as possible at supper. He'd gone up to their room, hoping to find her, but she hadn't been there either. The door to her attached dressing room had been locked, so he'd assumed she was inside and ignoring him. It had remained locked this morning, and not wanting to wake her, he'd gone down to the training yard—and proceeded to get his ass kicked by his grandfather.

That guy didn't mess around. Granted, Ian hadn't spent his whole life training with a sword. But still. He worked out religiously, always had. And yet, his grandfather had disarmed him so quickly he could still feel the vibration from the clash of metal ringing down his arm.

Admittedly, he'd been distracted.

He'd obviously messed up. Again. And he couldn't leave things the way they were. He needed to talk to Màiri.

So he'd left the training field, ignoring the taunts of his clansmen, and headed to the great hall. Surely she'd come down by now.

But there was no sign of her. Other than a few servants milling around, he only saw Marian sitting calmly before the hearth in the hall, knitting of all things. He hadn't ever seen her knit before.

She'd looked up and said calmly, "She's gone."

Which was when he'd promptly lost his shit.

In response to his rude comment, she clarified, "Gone. Left. Is no longer here."

"Where is she?"

Ian was trying to stay calm. But unlike Marian, he had no idea where the hell his wife had gone.

"She went home."

"Pardon, my lord." A servant stepped around him as they began to prepare for the midday meal. He could already smell meat roasting from the kitchen behind the hall. But Ian wasn't hungry. He was terrified.

"Home? Is she traveling alone? When did she leave? What did she say?"

Marian nodded to the wooden bench beside her.

Ian sat, heart hammering in his ears.

"She said it was your idea. You suggested she should not wait for Shona and the others to arrive."

"Tell me someone went with her."

"Alastair and two others."

Alastair. He'd not been in the training yard. At least she was safe. But Ian wasn't a complete idiot. He could see Marian was mad at him. It had been obvious from her first comment.

"We're family," he prompted. "Say what you're thinking."

Marian dropped whatever she was knitting in her lap.

"I'm thinking you and your brother have much in common. And that you're likely to regret your speech to Màiri, though it will be too late to fix what you've broken when you do."

His speech. "So she told you everything."

Marian reached up to push a strand of long blond hair behind her back. She stared into the fire for so long, Ian almost repeated the question.

"Aye, she did."

"I just wanted to protect her, Marian. It wasn't fair to keep her tethered to me anymore."

"She did not precisely see it that way."

Ian was going stir-crazy, although he couldn't say why. Màiri had done exactly what he'd suggested. But she'd done it without him. Was it wrong of him to have thought she'd at least say goodbye? They were married, after all. Kind of.

"How, precisely, did she see it?"

Ian didn't mean to be so short with Marian, but he couldn't help it. How was she so calm? His wife had literally left, without saying a word. He would never see her again. His shoulders sagged.

"She said, *Ian does not feel as I do. There's no reason for me to stay any longer.*"

His heart skipped a beat. "What does that mean? 'As I do'?"

Marian looked at him the same way Reik did whenever he asked his brother to go out. Sometimes he would actually agree, if only to leave the hell of his own thoughts, but he still always gave Ian that look.

"Surely you realize Màiri loves you?"

Ian swallowed. "I doubt it. We hardly know each other."

That look, still.

"She'll realize pretty quickly I'm not the only guy who can make her . . ." Yeah, he wasn't going to talk about orgasms with his sister-in-law. "Feel good."

Marian frowned, shaking her head. "Then perhaps it is for the best that she left. The others will be here any day. As you said, there is no reason for her to wait."

Marian picked up her knitting again and started where she'd left off. He watched the movement of her hands, but he didn't really see them. Numb, and not from his frozen toes, Ian didn't move. He thought of Màiri bundled up against the cold, riding next to Alastair, heading back to Kinross. What would she tell her father?

Ian had intended to go with her to ease the transition. Would she tell her father the truth? Would he believe it? Perhaps not.

Or maybe she would tell her father that Ian had sent her home. Laird Kelbrue could show up here asking for his head on a plate. Would that be such a bad thing? Maybe Màiri would come, too, and they could at least say goodbye.

Asshole.

Of course it would be a bad thing. Way to smooth over one clan rivalry and start a brand new one. He might even continue to withhold support from the Bruce out of spite because a MacKinnish had wronged his daughter.

That would be a serious problem—he knew that—but he also knew that wasn't what bothered him most. He hated the idea of never seeing Màiri again, her smile or that look of pure pleasure he'd put on her face.

"You're thinking of her?"

Grey's wife was persistent, to be sure.

"She'd have liked New Orleans," he said. The first time he'd dared to say it out loud, but not the first time he'd thought it. "No one would look at her strangely there. A birthmark on her cheek? If anything, she'd be embraced because of it. My city's history is steeped in acceptance, in some ways at least. We have a ways to go in others . . ."

Ian stopped rambling. He allowed himself, for just a second, to imagine Màiri sitting beside him at Muriel's as they talked about their joint venture, a nonprofit for—well, whatever cause she wanted to take up. He had so many ideas, none of which had anything to do with McCaim Shipping or public relations. At least not in the *putting out fires* sense.

Something compelled him to look up, to meet Marian's eyes.

"Did she tell you she loved me? Or did you just infer it?"

He was splitting hairs now.

"She was quite clear in her affections for you." Marian's perfectly shaped brows rose. "Your feelings for her are obvious as well."

His chest rose and fell as he struggled to get air in and out naturally.

"I care about her," he admitted.

Marian said nothing.

"And obviously I like her, in that way."

He was trying not to be crude. But honestly, Ian wasn't very accustomed to talking to women he wasn't trying to sleep with. It was strange, even more so to think Rhys was also married, to a woman he'd never met.

"Obviously," Marian said, mimicking his accent. He laughed, wondering if he sounded that bad whenever he tried to emulate theirs. Probably worse.

"And I want what's best for her," he continued. "She deserves so much."

Which was part of the reason he'd thought she would be better off without him. Ian thought of something then.

"Did she say anything about Ambrose?"

God, he was such an idiot. He'd actually encouraged her to marry him. No wonder she'd left without saying goodbye.

Marian didn't answer.

"Marian? Did she say anything about him?"

Still no answer. Instead, his sister-in-law sighed, as if the topic made her sad.

It felt like confirmation that Màiri had said something, that she was going to marry him. And it had all been his fucking idea.

"She's going to marry him, isn't she?" No way. "But she doesn't love him. It's so obvious. I mean, maybe she does, but she only cares for him as she would a brother. Not as a husband."

Ambrose would not make her scream out his name. If she married him, she would feel hollow. As if something was missing.

Much like he did right now.

"No, she can't," he said, getting to his feet and pacing in front of the hearth. "It's not a good idea."

"But"—Marian's hands paused—"'twas your idea. Màiri said as much."

Yeah, his idea. His really bad, no good, horrible idea.

"Did she say when she planned on going through with it? I mean, technically we're still married. She can't do it until I leave. It wouldn't be legal. And what if we can't get back? I have the cross, and the fact that we're here means it works. But . . ." He stopped, noticing for the first time what Marian was knitting.

"Is that . . . ?" His eyes widened. "Marian, is that sweater for a baby?"

Her eyes lit up.

"It is! Holy shit. You're pregnant. Does my brother know?"

Marian shook her head. "Nay, and please do not tell him. I will have this finished by tomorrow and plan to give it to him."

He couldn't stop smiling. They were going to have a baby in the family. He was going to be an uncle.

"Of course, I won't say a word. Congratulations. I'm so happy for you."

Ian hugged his sister-in-law, trying to imagine a tiny little baby in her stomach. How far along was she? Would it be a boy or a girl?

"Grey is going to be a father. Who would've thunk it."

His brother would make an amazing father. They'd had a great example.

"I'll see you later," he said, pulling away.

Marian didn't look surprised, just interested. "Where are you going?"

Where was he going? Great question. If only he knew.

"I need to clear my head."

But as he looked for the steward to fetch his mantle, Ian realized he did know. None of his brothers would argue with his self-assessment that he could be a total asshole, but Ian wasn't as thick as he'd made himself out to be these last few days.

He did know where he was going. And it wasn't for a walk to clear his head.

Ian was going to find his wife. And to tell her in no uncertain terms she would not be marrying Ambrose.

Because she was already married.

If Ian had believed in fate—and okay, maybe he did a little—he would say it made a hell of a lot of sense that they'd caught up with Màiri here, at the loch where it all had started. But the look she was giving him today wasn't at all inviting. She was downright pissed.

Which was no less than he deserved.

Ian winced every time he thought of the pretty speech he'd given her. What an ass. His only excuse was that he'd been scared. He was still scared. In many ways, Màiri was still a stranger. They still had so much to learn about each other. What was her favorite color? Her biggest fear?

"She doesn't look happy," he said to Grey.

"Yeah. I wonder why."

Knowing he'd be in for a tongue-lashing eventually anyway, he'd gone straight to his brother after leaving Marian. And Grey had been all too happy to accompany him, although he hadn't held back on the ride—he'd let Ian know exactly what he thought of his treatment of Màiri the night before.

Greeting his uncle Alastair, who didn't appear all that pleased to see him, Ian leapt off his horse. He tried to psych himself up with the thought that they might laugh about this someday—how two important moments in their life had happened by the same lake, the very one her father had drained to keep his enemy from fishing.

Except no one was laughing now. Least of all him. He held out his hand, and thankfully, she dismounted. Now that he stood opposite her, looking into her eyes, he could feel every bit of confidence drifting away. This was worse than anger. His wife looked sad. Defeated. As if the fight had gone out of her.

But it had not gone out of him.

"I am the biggest idiot on the planet. In your time and mine."

Remembering the others who weren't privy to their unique circumstances, he took a few steps closer to Màiri. Even her horse didn't want him near. The animal nickered and stamped its feet.

"I should never have said what I did."

His uncle stepped out in front of Màiri, a sour look on his face.

"Alastair," Grey called. Bless him.

His uncle didn't seem inclined to move, so he continued talking, stepping a little to the side so he could look into her eyes.

"Please," he said, lifting a hand up to his wife. "Please just listen to me. And then if you want to mount back up and ride to Kinross, I won't stop you. But we need to talk."

Màiri nodded to his uncle, as if he was her protector.

That should be him.

And he vowed it would be from this second forward.

Then she took Ian's hand, and in that moment he knew. He had suspected. He had questioned. He had thought it possible. And now he knew without a shadow of a doubt.

He loved his wife.

Even though she had not forgiven him, Ian felt as if he won the lottery. And the prize wasn't money. He had plenty of that.

It was the realization that he would never again have to question what it felt like to be in love.

It seemed like as good a place to start as any.

"I love you, Màiri."

Not surprisingly, she looked skeptical. What man was foolish enough to try to send the woman he loved into another man's arms?

This one, apparently.

"I honestly don't know what the hell I was thinking last night. After meeting Ambrose, I just thought . . . he's a good man. Better than me in a lot of ways. And you deserve a good man. Not a confused one who's always struggling to measure up. I thought I was doing you a favor. But then I talked to Marian, and when she told me how you felt . . . you can't marry him. You're already married to me."

That hadn't come out exactly as he'd planned.

"Marry Ambrose?"

"Yeah. I asked if you were planning to marry Ambrose, and Marian said . . ." What had she said precisely?

"She told you aye?"

He tried to remember.

"Actually, I don't know if she ever really answered."

Màiri cocked her head to the side as her horse protested again. Ian pulled her away before either of them could get hurt.

"Were you?" he asked. "Planning to marry him?"

One look into her eyes gave him the answer.

Shit. She hadn't intended to marry him at all. Marian had let him think it because she knew it would make him jealous. And of course it had worked. He was in love with this woman.

"Never mind. It wouldn't work."

"Nay?"

"Nay. Because you're married to me. And I want you to stay married to me. Come back home with me. I know it's a big decision. You'd have to leave your father, leave everything you know. But Màiri, I swear to God, I'll make you happy. We can come back to Scotland, visit your ancestors, whenever you want." He took her other hand. "Forgive me."

What if she told him to pound sand? What would he do if she got back on her horse and rode the rest of the way to Kinross?

Ian knew exactly what he would do.

"I'll stay. If you don't want to leave, I'll stay here. I'd miss my brothers like hell, but it's not fair for me to assume you'll come. Your call. But just say you'll stay married to me."

Ian held his breath, waiting.

Oh God, please don't say no.

"New Orleans does sound intriguing."

His heart soared.

"As do those been, bein . . ."

"Beignets. We can have them every single morning. Màiri, are you saying . . . ?" He couldn't finish. He simply couldn't.

"You broke my heart, to use an expression of yours. Last night, I thought to tell you . . ."

He kissed her. Ian couldn't wait any longer. He pulled his wife toward him and kissed the hell out of her, not even caring they had an audience who was clearly amused by their display.

"I am so very sorry."

"I packed my trunk for naught."

Ian wrapped his arms around her, beyond relieved that she'd recovered enough to tease him. "I love you so fucking much."

"I may have used that word to Marian last eve. But not quite in that way," Màiri admitted in his ear. He couldn't help but smile.

"Good. And you can use it again if I ever act like such an asshole."

He paused.

"So you'll come back? To Hightower," he clarified, not wanting to push her on a decision to leave Scotland. As he'd said, it was a huge decision, and he wanted Màiri to have some time to think on it. Unfortunately, they may only have a few days. But the choice was hers, and he intended to honor whatever decision she made.

"You'll remain my wife?"

Màiri's smile was even more radiant than the loch beside them.

"I will."

Ian kissed her again, realizing something important. "If we're staying married"—his eyes narrowed—"you do know what that means, don't you?"

But his wife clearly had no idea what he was talking about. Thankfully, he could show her soon enough.

"It means I can show you the most important meaning of your favorite new word. The minute we get back to the castle."

This promised to be the longest ride of his life.

26

"YOU HAVE NOTHING TO WORRY ABOUT."

Màiri grasped Marian's hands. "Thank you. For your kindness, for listening to me, and"—she smiled coyly—"for making Ian believe I would marry Ambrose."

Marian squeezed back. "The man could not—what was the expression Grey used? Ah, yes. He could not see the nose in front of his face. 'Twas evident he loved you, but he was scared to admit it."

"You said nothing of it when I left."

Màiri paused, listening for any movement in the adjoining chamber. Nothing yet.

"I thought it might create a little more urgency if you left as you did. 'Twas a good decision."

"But not one made for that purpose." She truly had intended to go home. Every moment of the ride had been spent in contemplation of what she would tell her father. Would he believe the truth? Likely not, especially if Ian and the others did not leave for a while, but anything less would mean inevitable war with Clan MacKinnish. Even so, being around Ian had become unbearable.

And then, when she'd seen him approaching the loch . . .

"To think so many husbands and wives spend a lifetime together but never find love," she said.

"Do you believe 'twas meant to be this way? That Shona was pulled back through time so that her sons might find us? And that their intervention actually makes things play out the way they do instead of changing history?"

"How can we ever know?"

Marian frowned. "I suppose we cannot. Mayhap 'twill become clearer once we return to their time."

She paused. Màiri had told her of Ian's offer.

"Have you given it more thought?"

Leaving her father and Alana forever or tearing Ian away from his family. It was a decision she'd prefer not to make, but one that would haunt her these next few days. Though she longed to see the future Ian had described to her, how could she leave her family knowing war was coming? Knowing it seemed likely her father would sire a son that would play a large part in that war?

"Aye," was all she said for now. The adjoining door opened, ending any more conversation about her future. Ian stood there, hair still partially wet. Wearing a long linen shirt with a wide opening at his chest, along with braies and boots, Ian looked completely different than he had earlier at supper. But it was not only his dress that was different.

He seemed relaxed. Happy.

Would he be so if she decided they should stay?

"I'll be needing my wife now."

She and Marian exchanged a glance. It occurred to her that if she stayed, she'd be parted from her new friend forever.

Either way, she'd be leaving someone she cared about.

"Thank you," she said, moving toward the bedchamber.

Màiri heard the click of the door as Marian left the dressing chamber. Her friend had assured her she had nothing to worry about. That, however impossible it seemed that she and Ian should fit together in such a way, it would in fact work.

Ian handed her a goblet of wine.

"Drink this."

She took it from him, taking a long sip as she crossed the threshold. Màiri's eyes widened. The chamber was full of warm light, from the roaring fire and candles placed strategically around the space. Pansies were everywhere. Beautiful winter ones, purple and gold.

"Two of the three colors of New Orleans."

Was that an appeal for her to make up her mind? Pushing the thought aside, she took another step, inhaling. "I can smell them," she said, taking another sip of wine. "'Tis beautiful."

Ian moved toward the fire, motioning for her to join him. It was warmer in here, even more so near the flames. Màiri's best shift, though beautifully embroidered, did nothing to provide her warmth.

Ian placed his own goblet on the wooden table. Stooping to remove his boots, he then reclaimed the goblet and walked back toward her. His tunic had hung down, giving her a glimpse of his chest as he bent over, but she averted her gaze at the last moment, pretending she hadn't noticed.

"I saw you peeking."

She smiled.

"If you do not practice with swords or other weapons, how do you look so?"

Ian sipped from his own goblet, seemingly content to stand before the fire with her for now.

"It's called the gym. Kind of hard to explain, but you work your muscles in there, simulating the kind of workout you'd get in the training yard."

A strange concept indeed.

"What are some of the other differences between our times?"

Màiri didn't know how long they stood there, exchanging

stories. But after two helpings of wine, she was feeling a bit more relaxed.

When she finished the second, Ian took both of their goblets and placed them on the table. His look, unmistakable. She'd seen it before and knew where it would lead. But this time, there would be nothing to stop them from consummating their marriage at last.

"Are you still nervous?"

"Aye."

He closed the gap between them, his finger lifting her chin. "Look at me."

She did.

"You will get more pleasure than pain. And after tonight, there will never be pain again. I promise."

He kissed her then, and it was an entirely different kiss from their frantic reunion earlier in the day. His lips covered hers, slowly, as if they had the entire evening to explore. Which of course, they did.

She opened for him, Ian's tongue gliding into her mouth, tasting her as she did him. When his hands ran from her hips up toward her breasts, she placed her hands on his shoulders.

Cupping her, Ian rubbed her nipples through her shift, eliciting a moan from her. He continued to kiss her, so slowly that Màiri found she wanted just the opposite. A fire burned within her, and this languorous pace would not do.

Màiri thought of being bold, but it was difficult to cast aside a lifetime of sermons about the proper place of a woman.

And yet . . . Ian had insisted there should be no shame between a husband and wife. So, pretending they were, indeed, in the future, Màiri reached her hand between them.

It was hard, just as it had been that day.

Ian's groan was her first hint that she had done something right. Her second? Just as she'd intended, his slow kiss deepened and became more insistent. When she felt his hands on her thighs, Màiri knew what he intended before her shift was lifted over her head.

"You as well," she said, breaking away.

Ian complied, lifting his shirt and tossing it aside. When he reached for her, their bodies pressed together, Màiri's sigh of pleasure was swallowed by a very different kind of kiss. So engulfed by sensation, she didn't even realize he'd moved them toward the bed until she felt it behind her legs. Lifting her, Ian placed her on the very edge. She attempted to move back, toward the pillow, but his hands on her thighs stayed her.

Then, opening her legs, he squatted below her on the ground. This time, more prepared than the last, she did not attempt to close her legs. Giving her husband complete access, Màiri was rewarded as his tongue expertly licked, his lips revering her in a way she hadn't thought possible. His hands gripped her thighs, and Màiri found herself grasping his hair with her hands, pulling him closer and closer yet.

She couldn't help the moans that escaped, and Ian urged her not to try. And when she exploded, he moved quickly, lying her back onto the bed.

When had he undressed?

Making room for him, her core still pulsing, Màiri was too dazed to worry about how this might work. When Ian leaned down, his mouth covering her breast, she held on and attempted to catch her breath.

It was only when she felt his hand between them, opening her and . . .

"'Twill not fit," she couldn't help but explain, despite the deep sense of pleasure that coursed through every bit of her.

"It will." Ian lifted his head. "Can you feel how easily we come together?"

He pressed into her, slowly. Gently.

"You're wet, so ready for me. I'm almost there."

"Almost where?"

And then, without warning, he thrust through the only barrier between them. Of course that's what he had meant. And it did hurt. She squeezed his shoulders in pain, but with Ian's lips on hers, she did forget it for a moment.

Màiri kissed him back with everything she had, and when Ian started to move again, she realized the pain was already gone. It had been replaced with a fullness like nothing she'd ever felt. Before long, she was actually encouraging him to thrust deeper.

Faster.

He broke away, and she was glad for it. Màiri wanted to see his face, wanted to know what he was thinking. And when she met his eyes, it was clearer than any words could be.

He loved her.

Desired her, aye. But loved her as well. Màiri felt it deep inside of her. As Ian moved quicker, his hand ventured between them, rubbing and circling.

"Ian." She had nothing else to say but that.

"I know. God, Màiri, I know."

When he pressed into her this time, she could not hold on. Pushing her hips up into her husband, she felt a more powerful release than she'd yet experienced.

When he called her name, she told him to say it again.

Over and over he said it, until he lay atop her, whispering it softly into her ear.

"That"—he kissed her ear— "is what we call making love in my time."

He closed his eyes then, propping himself above her. When he opened them, he shook his head a little, as if in disbelief, and looked at her with wonder.

"Hmmm," she murmured, content to gaze up at this beautiful man, now her husband in truth. "I thought you said 'twas called something else."

Ian laughed.

"Fucking. Is that what you meant?"

She nodded.

"Yeah, I thought so too. But not that. Not with you."

Màiri wasn't sure she understood the difference. But she didn't care what it was called. She wanted to do it again.

27

"MARRIED," Grey taunted him. "In love? Has time travel addled your brain?"

They were the exact words Ian had said to Grey a few weeks previously. Apparently he was never going to live this down.

They'd finished training for the day. Although Ian and his brother were unlikely to take part in any future battles, they joined their uncles and their grandfather each day in the fields, something the men did to prepare for any trouble the clan might encounter. Once the McCaims left Hightower, some would stay here and others would be sent on various missions either at their grandfather's or their allies' behest.

Behest. He was even thinking like a medieval now.

And even though the last two days with his wife had been among the happiest in his life, the arrival of his family loomed.

So much could go wrong.

He'd been insulated here, but he didn't need Grey to tell him they'd come to a dangerous place. This training might be nothing more than a good workout for them, but for the others, it truly was life and death.

Just yesterday they'd been called to intervene in a skirmish in the village between two men. One had accused the other of stealing the laird's sheep. For this offense, he'd stolen the other man's wife. Ian had thought Alastair was joking about that, but sure enough, they'd ridden out to the remote structure where she was being held and rescued the poor woman.

And this sort of infighting was child's play compared to the antics between rival clans. Never mind the whole Bruce versus Balliol versus the Guardians of Scotland versus the king of England affair that was brewing. Leave it to Rhys and Reik to get themselves caught up in that mess.

His grandfather said something to him as he handed his sword to the armorer. Ian couldn't hear what he'd yelled, exactly, but it couldn't be good. He'd failed to disarm Ian for the first time today, and the old man was still smarting over his slip.

Although he still couldn't hope to best his grandfather or uncles in a swordfight, Ian had learned to get away from them easily enough. He had even managed to bring the tip of his sword to his Uncle Colban's back. Once. Before the man spun and blocked Ian's efforts.

Still. It was something.

"Do you really think she might decide to stay?" he asked, waving to their grandfather cheerfully as he and Grey stepped inside the keep. "We have to talk about this."

"No," his brother said, stopping in a deserted corridor. "We do not."

A staring contest ensued. Ian won every time. But Grey must have learned a thing or two thanks to his time with Ross, otherwise known as the Viking, because he lasted a lot longer than he normally did. Still, Ian could outstare the best of them, and Grey finally blinked.

"Damn you."

Ian chuckled.

"You can't stay."

He knew that tone. Grey didn't get emotional often, but

when he did, it was obvious—at least to Ian. Maybe a sign of things to come as Greyson became a father?

"I thought you didn't want to talk about it?"

Grey shuffled his weight from one foot to the other. Ian had made a career of watching for clues. Reading body language. He didn't blame his brother for being nervous. Ian was scared as hell Màiri might ask to stay. And she would be within her rights to do so. He had, after all, offered.

"I can't believe you suggested it," Grey admitted. And his tone revealed what Ian had already known—Grey was pissed about it.

"How could I not? Unlike Marian, she has family here. I can't presume her family is less important to her than ours is to us."

"Marian had family here too."

Ian made a sound in his throat. "Yeah, a father who tried to marry her off to some Scottish noble dickhead. Nice guy."

What would Grey have done if his wife *did* have family here she loved and wanted to be with . . . Would he leave her? Force her to leave them? They both knew the answer, but his brother wouldn't admit it.

"If she wants to stay, it would kill me, Grey," he said, his voice breaking a little. "You know that. I'm the most sentimental of the bunch."

They all knew that was true. His brother couldn't deny it.

"Not knowing if Dad was OK. Not to mention it would screw with my head royally to know you don't even technically exist yet."

The idea of it baffled them both. Normally, they just didn't talk about the strange paradoxes of time travel.

It occurred to him that it was probably time for him to bring up something else they didn't talk about. If he and Màiri *did* go back to New Orleans, would he really step back into the role he hated? No. It wouldn't be right to ask her to step out of her comfort zone if he was too much of a coward to be real with the people in his life. Fuck it. Time to grow up.

"I don't belong there."

Grey just stared at him. It took him a solid thirty seconds to say, "In the future?"

Ian thought of their home. The food. The music. The flushing toilets. Fuck no, he definitely belonged in the future. He loved New Orleans almost as much as he loved his family.

"No. I mean at McCaim."

He couldn't believe he was finally saying this. But it had to be said.

"When Dad first told us about his plans for the company, our roles in it, everyone assumed I would handle our public relations."

Grey frowned. "Because you love that shit."

"*Loved.* Back in college. But who the hell knows what they really like in college? Or what they want to do for the rest of their lives?"

He thought of his brothers, all of whom had seemed to know that very thing.

"Don't answer that."

He expected his brother to look confused. To ask questions. To flip out. Instead, he just shook his head, his lips pressed together. As if . . .

As if he already knew.

"It's about time, asshole," Grey said at last.

Ian's mouth dropped open.

"Mom told you?" He couldn't believe his mother had betrayed his confidence. She'd promised to keep their conversation to herself, and besides, he hadn't even told her the extent of his dissatisfaction.

"Mom? No. She didn't say a word. I'm your brother. We are your brothers."

"We?"

"Yeah, we. Rhys. Reik. Me. We all know PR isn't really for you. At least not with McCaim."

He couldn't believe what he was hearing. "But you never said anything."

"What were we supposed to say? 'Hey, how about you get a job somewhere else?' As if you wouldn't have taken that the wrong way."

Kind of like the way he'd reacted when his mom had talked to him about it. Ian had jumped to the conclusion that she didn't have confidence in him. But really, he didn't have confidence in himself.

"You could have, I don't know, played guidance counselor or something. Asked a few questions. Maybe hinted that you wouldn't be pissed if I wanted to do something else."

"The only guidance counselor in our family disappeared five years ago. The rest of us schmucks have been on autopilot ever since. It's what made the company so successful."

"Made?"

Grey sighed. "We've got to do things a bit differently from now on. If we'd slowed down a bit, we might have realized Dad was onto something. We might have listened."

"About time travel?"

The bell for vespers sounded. Mass, the meal—all of it would have to wait. He and his brother were having a come-to-Jesus moment, and no one was more surprised than Ian at this particular turn of events.

"I mean, maybe?"

Ian didn't think so. After all, it was *time travel*. But his brother had a point.

"Ian, why were you so worried to say something? I mean, we figured you couldn't hate it that much since you never said a word."

He knew what Grey meant. Ian was usually the sociable one. The extrovert. The baby brother without a care in the world.

Except he did have one. More than one. And being left out of the "club" was probably his biggest fear. He never said so aloud, but Ian was desperate to feel he belonged. He wanted to be one of the McCaim boys more than all three of his brothers put together.

"I . . ." He wasn't sure how to put all of that into words. "I don't know."

Grey looked at him. And then pulled him in close. Two hugs in as many weeks. His mother would be so proud of them.

Ian clung to his brother, fighting back tears. He should have said all of that sooner. But he'd been so afraid of what they might say, how they might interpret it.

"I don't want to lose you guys, again."

Grey tightened his grip. "I don't want to lose you either. But whatever you decide, whether it's to stay here or come back and make your own way—" He pushed Ian back, looking into his eyes. And this time, Grey didn't turn away. "—I love you. *We* love you. Nothing will change that, brother. Ever."

Ian couldn't answer him. But he did look away first, giving Grey his first-ever staring contest victory. His brother's laughter was a clear cover-up for an emotion that made them both uncomfortable. But one they'd gotten plenty of practice with over the last year.

But soon, he hoped to God, it would all be over. The question was, how exactly would this nightmare turned adventure of a lifetime end?

"You've not been hiding it."

Ian ran his finger along her cheek. Màiri stretched out on the bed, content to breathe in the scent of him. To wonder which part of her he would explore next. Though they'd been married, truly married, Ian did not seem inclined to cease his explorations, for which she was grateful.

But now he looked at her cheek. This gesture was, in some ways, more intimate than some of the others. Ones Màiri doubted she could ever speak about to anyone, even Marian. He might claim it was natural, nothing about which to be ashamed, but Màiri could feel her cheeks pinken at the thought of it.

"Nay, I don't try to hide it anymore," she countered, turning on her side to face him. She pulled the coverlet with her, but Ian pushed it back down.

"And definitely don't hide those."

She swatted his hand playfully. "You said my body is mine and mine alone."

Ian's eyes narrowed. "Maybe we should have skipped those discussions on women's rights. I should have never brought it up."

She knew Ian was not serious. But she pulled the coverlet back up anyway just to torment him.

When he stopped wallowing, she relented, giving him the view he'd been coveting.

"You're a quick study." His hand moved from Màiri's mark down her neck, his finger tracing a sensuous path downward.

"You know," she said, "only you and Alana have ever talked to me about hiding my mark. Father has never mentioned it once."

"Because, for all his gruffness, your father is a kind and gentle man. He wouldn't want to hurt your feelings."

"You and Alana both mentioned it."

Ian's fingers began to stray farther downward. "People have different ways of loving."

Not surprisingly, his hand found the very spot she'd just uncovered.

"My father maybe said the words five times in my life that I can remember," he continued. "My mom, literally every day. But I know Dad loves me and my brothers just as much as Mom. He just shows it differently."

Màiri would have a difficult time continuing this discussion if Ian did not cease his ministrations. Now his thumb ran across her nipple, turning it into a hard peak. She watched his eyes, filled now with desire, and tried to attend to their discussion.

"My father would be devastated to lose me. 'Twas why I thought he might set aside his rivalry with Clan Dern to marry me to Ambrose, who lived so close."

They'd carefully avoided discussing their future these past few days, but her decision hung over them all. Not just her and Ian, but Grey and Marian too. Colban had admitted that he would be overjoyed for them to stay, to have his sister's son in their midst.

Every time she saw Ian with his brother, she opened her mouth to tell him she'd do it. She would go to the future with him. Experience the changes Ian talked about. Healthcare. Women's rights. Potentially, a longer life. But then a vision of her father, alone, his daughter gone forever, his young yet unborn son, off fighting in a war that would prove never-ending . . . it held her back.

Closing her eyes, Màiri tried to stop thinking of it as she lay her head on the pillow and enjoyed the sensation of Ian's lips closing around her breast as his hand strayed lower. It was so easy to give over to the sensations he awoke in her.

"Ian," she murmured as his teeth gently nipped at her. A jolt between her legs demanded what he was now giving as his hand ran inward from her thigh.

"Mmm," was his only response.

Suddenly, he was everywhere. His lips, his tongue . . . his fingers. She giggled, startling him, as she remembered the word he'd used for what he was doing just now.

Versatile, indeed.

"Not the response I was hoping for," he said, lifting his head.

As she loved to do, Màiri ran her hand through his thick hair. In response, he edged closer, capturing her lips in a searing kiss. She gave over to him swiftly and without hesitation. One moment, his hand was between them. The next, her husband had flipped them over, Màiri now above him as they'd done the night before.

Guiding himself into her, Ian moved his hips, his hands covering her breasts. And this time, she made love to him. This position felt a little different. She was powerful and in control, and his expression left no doubt he enjoyed it as much as she.

When she felt the spasms take her, Ian's moans echoing in her ears, Màiri collapsed against him. Her husband circled his arms around her, holding her tightly to his chest, and Màiri suddenly had the urge to cry. What an odd response.

"I know the difference now," she said, not loosening their embrace. "Between making love and . . ."

A sharp knock at the door interrupted her. This was no ordinary knock. Màiri jumped up as Ian scrambled off the bed. His reaction left little doubt that he sensed what she did. Something was wrong.

"Ian," Grey shouted. "Open up."

"Hold on," Ian called back, dressing. Màiri picked her shift up off the floor, slipping it over her head.

"Ian," his brother called again, knocking as if his brother hadn't responded.

Màiri's heart thudded in response. Were they under attack? Had someone been injured?

Unlocking the door, Ian whipped it open. Greyson's expression confirmed what they'd already suspected. Something had happened.

She had never seen Ian's brother look this way before. He'd always seemed so in control. But not now, not at this moment.

"They're here."

29

"Go," Màiri said, running to the side of the bed, grabbing his shirt and handing it to him.

"I'll wait for you," he said in a fog.

But Màiri pushed him away. "Go. I will be along."

So he did, running after his brother. They'd probably break their necks in these corridors, darkness having fallen hours before, but he couldn't bring himself to care.

"I haven't been down there yet," Grey said in front of him. "A servant came to our chamber and I ran straight here."

Ian couldn't get down to the hall fast enough. They navigated the narrow staircase, descending the tower like they were eight-year-olds at the Mardi Gras parade, scrambling for doubloons tossed from the floats.

"It's so late," he muttered. Of all the nonsensical things, he found himself worrying about his brothers riding through the dark. But of course it didn't matter—they were here. "What did he say?"

They raced through the mostly sleeping castle.

"Just to come quick. Your brothers have arrived."

Your brothers. Only their grandfather, their uncles, and a

few others knew their true identities. Everyone else believed the stories that he and Grey were the sons of Laird MacKinnish's sister-in-law. Those who'd known Shona well enough to recognize her, despite her age, had been told the truth when she was last at Hightower. But she'd kept a low profile, not eating most of her meals in the hall, keeping to herself. To be cautious.

"Brothers," he repeated, his heart racing as they turned the final corner. "Plural."

Rhys and Reik. They were both here.

Then they turned a corner into the hall, and there they were. Standing in the hall like two Clan MacKinnish warriors, looking both different and the same.

Ian froze, not believing his eyes.

Rhys was the one who moved first. He ran to the two of them, somehow managing to pull them both into a hug at the same time.

They had an audience, all of the servants who slept in the hall plus their grandfather. Ian didn't see his uncles yet. Other men, both hooded, also accompanied them.

"God, it's good to see you two."

Rhys pulled away, but he held each one of them by the necks. "Mom's fine. I'll explain what happened when we're alone," he whispered.

Another arm grasped him from behind. He knew it well, had been headlocked by Reik more times than he could count.

He still couldn't believe it. They were really here. Safe. Alive. He would have been shaking if not for the three hulking figures around him, steadying him. As always.

Ian might have spent his life hating his role as the family baby, but right now he loved it. Wanted to be held like a two-year old. Wanted his brothers to be stronger than him. Because he was seriously close to losing it.

Get a grip, Ian. These people are going to think you're all crazy.

"We'll tell them we haven't seen each other in a year." That comment was from Reikart.

Pulling away, the four of them looked at one another, Rhys bursting into laughter. "Look at us."

Ian did, shaking his head in wonder. They were really here, together. Finally. All in one place.

"It's a good look. Especially on you," he said to Rhys. His older brother had always had the bearing of a leader, a warrior, likely the product of being the firstborn. But now, if possible, he had a new confidence that Ian hadn't seen in him before.

"Are you smiling?" Grey asked Reik.

Ian shifted his attention to Reikart, and sure enough, his brother was doing just that. Sometimes, over the last few years, he'd wondered if Reik even knew how to smile anymore. But apparently a family reunion did wonders for a person.

Or was it something more?

Ian finally noticed his brothers' traveling companions. They'd been bundled up from head to toe, but now they were handing their mantles to a servant, and Ian could clearly see they were both women.

The beautiful redhead could only be Maggie. Although Grey hadn't met her, he'd heard about her from their mother. But there was another woman with her. A blonde, like Grey's wife. His eyes met Reik's.

Could it be possible? Had all four of them found wives?

"Bring food and wine. Come. All of you."

That decree came from their grandfather. Had Rhys and Reikart met him yet? Apparently they had, for his grandfather slapped Rhys on the back. "We move this reunion to my solar."

Just like the day their grandfather and Uncle Dermot had arrived. Only tonight Ian was so wound up he didn't even remember walking there. Nor did he pay attention to the servant bringing food to them, or anything other than his brothers' expressions. Like a kid who'd lost his parents in

Disney World, Ian stared at them, afraid they might disappear again if he took his eyes off either of them.

"Did Mom really go back?" he asked the second the last serving girl left the chamber.

Ross and Colban pulled benches and wooden chairs from their spots, arranging them in front of the hearth, and everyone took a seat.

"We have a lot to tell you," Rhys said. Ian wasn't patient by nature, but he tried like hell.

Reikart cleared his throat and glanced to the petite blonde, who'd sat next to him. "This is Deirdre Irvine McCaim, *my wife*."

Rhys and Reikart exchanged a quick look, and Rhys spoke next.

"Deirdre is Maggie's sister," Rhys said. "Maggie is *my wife*." The stunning redhead set a hand on his shoulder and smiled tentatively at Grey and Ian.

Ian frowned. "I don't know much about the situation, but I thought Deirdre was a traitor."

He flashed an apologetic look at the woman and her sister.

"'Tis understandable," Deirdre said, "but nay."

"Dee and I went to the English Court and got Aunt Grace's second cross back," Reik said. He frowned. "Did you guys know about the second cross?"

Ian nodded. "Alastair told us."

"When we arrived back at Lochlavine with the cross, as you must know, Mom was there. The three of us—Mom, Rhys, and I —decided she had to go back immediately to Dad."

She was really gone.

He understood the logic, but part of him had hoped that Alastair might have gotten it wrong. He'd wanted to see her, goddammit. If Màiri chose to stay, he'd never see her again.

Grey must have had the same thought. He caught his brother's eye and shook his head. Not yet. They'd discuss it later.

"I guess time travel has been good to all of us." Grey stood up, heading to the door. "I'll be back."

He left, Rhys and Reik staring after him. They were undoubtedly wondering where he'd gone, but Ian didn't have to ask.

"He's gone for our wives."

"Your..."

Reik's look of shock was officially his favorite part of their reunion so far. It wasn't easy to surprise his brother.

Rhys wasn't so tactful.

"You've got to be shitting me."

Ian stretched his legs in front of him, crossing his arms. He was rarely in a position of power over his brothers, knowing something they didn't.

"Don't you mean shiting? You've picked up a bit of a brogue, brother."

Ross, despite having eaten supper already, had served himself from the tray. Mouth full, he made a sound. Everyone stopped to stare, Alastair breaking the silence.

"You've somethin' to say, brother?" he said to Ross. He was teasing him, and it struck Ian for the first time that their MacKinnish uncles had a connection a lot like theirs. They might be older, and from a time and place very different than their own, but their bond was the same.

"Mom told us about Grey, but you? I don't believe it." Rhys exchanged an incredulous glance with Reik.

"Màiri is the daughter of the laird of a neighboring clan," Ian said.

"Dern doesn't have a daughter. It must be Kelbrue," Reik said, surprising Ian with his knowledge of the local goings-on. But it shouldn't have surprised him. In some ways, Reik was the smartest of them all.

"Ask 'em how they met," his grandfather cut in. Everyone in the chamber laughed, except for his brothers and Dermot. Ian would prefer not to relay the story, but apparently he had no choice. They all looked at him in anticipation.

"We met near the loch," he said, sitting up. Rhys and Reik waited, but he was done with his story. It was all they'd be getting from him.

"They met when Ian kissed the lass before he even asked for her name," his grandfather supplied. "Then he told her father, who demanded they wed."

Rhys whistled. "Leave it to Ian to come through time with a bang."

He cleared his throat. "There's a bit more to it than that."

Actually, a lot more to it, including his wife's family, who would play an integral part in the history his brothers spoke of, a family Màiri was rightfully reluctant to leave.

Yes, there was more to it than they could possibly imagine. It killed him to consider parting from his brothers, but he wasn't the same man that had been dropped at the foot of Hightower Castle. Ian had to step up, even if it tore his heart out.

30

"Ian, don't do this."

They'd entertained his concerns earlier, but now that everyone else had gone off to bed and only the four of them remained awake and in their grandfather's solar, his big brothers were ganging up on him. More than a pitcher or two of ale later, they'd started berating and pleading with him in turns. Maybe he kind of liked the fact that they were so pissed off. Even though they were his brothers, and Ian knew without a doubt they loved him, it still felt good to have all three of them begging him to reconsider. It made him feel the love.

But he couldn't do it.

"She'll agree to it for my sake. So I can see Mom again. Find out if Dad's okay. I can't believe you guys, of all people, can't see this from my point of view. Your wives all want to go. It makes sense for them, but Màiri's worried about leaving her father. Would you have me take her away from him forever?"

Grey, drunk as a skunk, heaved a laugh. "Who says it's forever? We haven't talked about this, but we have the cross. Two of them, given Mom has the other. They're like plane tickets that don't expire."

All three of them looked at him, their eyes gleaming.

"What?" He shook his head, having thought it out already. "No way. That's not an option. I won't promise her we can come back. It's too risky."

"Staying here at the start of a long and bloody war isn't risky?" Rhys looked as if he could be on a Braveheart poster, minus the war paint.

"Jesus, you look different," Ian said, shaking his head.

"No, I don't."

"And how would you know? Did you bring a mirror back with you?"

"OK, that's enough," Reik, ever the mediator, broke in. "You're coming back with us. End of story. Grey's right. If Màiri is worried about leaving her father, you can visit. There's no reason to think it won't work."

Ian sat up straighter, looked his brother in the eyes, and put it all out there. "Maybe. Maybe not. But if I do . . ." He looked at Grey, who nodded. "I'll be getting a new job."

The look on Rhys's face almost made him reconsider. He wasn't angry, exactly, and he definitely wasn't as surprised as Ian would have expected before talking to Grey. Actually, if he were being honest, it wasn't Rhys's expression that gave him pause. It was the idea that he might be the only McCaim brother not to work in the company. That he'd be the odd man out.

"I'm only still there because of you. Because of Dad. But every day that goes by, I feel more and more hollow. As if I'm missing my calling and time is running out." He shrugged, trying to minimize the effect of his words. "I guess I'm the black sheep of the family."

Reik snorted. "If there's a black sheep, it's not you."

Rhys pulled his legs up under him and leaned forward. "No one here is surprised, least of all me. It sucks. You're damn good at your job. But you're right, it's not you."

"If you come back," Reik added, "why don't you start a

nonprofit? McCaim could do more than donate a few dollars here and there."

A few dollars was actually millions of dollars in charity. But Reik was right. Throwing money at problems didn't necessarily solve them. More finesse was needed.

"I have a few ideas," he admitted. "But I wanted to talk to Màiri about it too."

"If she decides to go."

He ignored Grey's hint of sarcasm. "Right. If she decides to go." He looked around the room, pausing for a moment on each of their faces. Looking for any signs of judgement or anger. "You really don't care?"

"I mean, we care. But we all like our jobs. You don't. Big difference." Reik took a swig from his mug. "After all we've been through, if we make it back in one piece . . ."

He didn't say it, but they all knew what he'd left unsaid. *If Mom is there. If Dad is alive.*

"We'll figure it out. Either way, you're a McCaim. That's all that matters."

He was a McCaim.

The youngest of four brothers, the son of a great man and a woman who had not only endured being separated from her family but being tossed hundreds of years into the future. And finally, though it had taken twenty-seven years for him to get there, his own man.

Ian smiled, raising his mug. "To the McCaim brothers. Now husbands, all a bit stronger, and at least one of us, still good-looking."

They raised their mugs in unison and drank.

"Kind of you to compliment me," Reik said. If he wanted to claim it, Ian would let him. He liked this version of his brother a hell of a lot more and would have to thank Deirdre when he saw her next.

He still had so many questions. When would they go through? Would he be with them? But for now he was just grateful for this moment, and for the strange twists of fate that had brought them here together.

31

Màiri was, as Ian would say, a nervous wreck.

"You guys ready?" Rhys asked.

Two days after his brothers' arrival, they all stood in a circle in Laird MacKinnish's solar, the cross cradled in Reik's hand. Màiri was most surprised to see Laird MacKinnish's eyes glistening. Aside from her father, he was the most stalwart man she knew, but Màiri would admit, these were very special circumstances.

A family was being torn apart. Two, actually. And although each of the brothers had traveled back in time once before, and Rhys and Reik had seen their mother make the journey, none of them really knew what to expect. All four brothers had landed back here in different places. Would that happen to them? What if they ended up in different times? Only their mother had gone through twice, but she didn't understand how it worked any better than they did.

Some things come down to fate, she'd said.

Which was the sentiment they had ultimately decided to embrace after two days of talking and planning that could easily come to naught once they said the chant. They were as ready as they would ever be.

Màiri looked at her father who had been just brought into the fold the day before and clasped Ian's hand.

They'd said their goodbyes, and she was ready to travel to the future.

Her father had made two promises.

First, to reconsider an alliance with the Bruce. Now that he was at least communicating with the laird of Clan Dern again, perhaps it would be easier for him to relent.

The second promise was one Màiri had exacted from him. Although Alana wasn't here, much to Màiri's dismay, her father had given his word to open his heart to her. Alana loved him, and her father, faced with the possibility he'd never see his daughter again, had admitted he felt the same way. She only wished she could have met a brother not yet born.

"Ready," they said, one by one.

But she wasn't, not really. Màiri could tell her father did not expect anything to happen. Even Shona's brothers looked skeptical, despite knowing everything they did about time travel. She suspected they were, as Reik had said, *in for a shock.*

She exchanged a glance with Marian, who appeared as nervous as she.

"Ready," they both murmured at the same time.

They weren't taking any chances. Every one of them had practiced the chant, over and over again, until all of the brothers had agreed they were saying it the right way.

"I love you," she said again to her father.

"And I love you, *mhuirnín.*"

"Thank you," Rhys said to Alastair and Dermot, who stood together, watching them carefully.

If only Ian had been able to meet his aunt Grace. But she'd had unfinished business to attend to, something important to do with the Fae who'd given her the crosses.

"Be well, nephew," Dermot responded for them both. Alastair, always the most tenderhearted of the MacKinnish brothers, remained silent. His smile was his only answer.

"I'm a better man because of you," Grey said to Ross. "Remember what I said."

Ross winked. Màiri wasn't sure what Grey had told his uncle, but his smile told her it meant something special to the man.

"On the count of three," Rhys said as each of them grabbed a piece of the cross. Despite the unnatural cold that emanated from the metal, it was hard to imagine this silver object would take them to the future. Still, Màiri could not doubt the power of the Fae, or the truth of what the cross had already done.

Some things were just not meant to be understood by all.

"Ian, lad," Laird MacKinnish said, "tell my daughter she did a fine job with all four sons."

Ian swallowed hard, unable to answer. She could tell it meant something to him that his grandfather had singled him out for this message. Ian, who'd always felt left out, had been accepted, not only as a McCaim but as a MacKinnish. He nodded in answer, taking a deep breath.

"One," Rhys said.

Màiri's heart raced. Maggie and Deirdre and Marian looked so calm in comparison. Did they feel as she did?

"Two."

Màiri smiled at her father one last time and then met her husband's eyes, Ian giving her all the reassurance she needed.

"Three."

They all spoke at once. "*Talamh, èadhar, teine, usige ga thilleadh dhachaigh.*"

32

IAN OPENED HIS EYES, his stomach swirling just like the first time. Except there was no snow under him because they were back in his father's study. His head snapped to the left . . . and there she was. He tried to sit up, to pull Màiri toward him, but his head pounded miserably. At least he caught a glimpse of Rhys next to her.

Ian tried to call out, to ask if everyone had made it through, but his throat felt like he'd just come down with a massive case of strep. He didn't remember that from the first time. Apparently no two time travel journeys were exactly alike. Go figure.

"Ian?"

Grey's voice. He tried to sit up again, and this time his body allowed it. Scanning the room quickly, he found . . . everyone. His brothers. Their wives. All of them made it through, and they were in his father's study, which looked much as they'd left it.

Holy shit!

"Everyone's here," he said, leaning toward Màiri. She was just opening her eyes now. He grabbed her, only belatedly realizing that she might not feel the best. But his own stomach was settling. Maybe she felt okay too.

"Màiri, are you all right?"

She opened her mouth and then promptly closed it. Moans and a few more yelled names announced their traveling party was finally coming to.

"It won't last long," he said, loosening his hold. At least, he hoped it wouldn't. "In a few minutes, you'll just feel a bit groggy, like you didn't get enough sleep."

"Fuck me," Reik said—what they were all likely thinking. All eight of them. Together. What were the chances?

Ian looked down to see the cross at Rhys's feet. It had come through with them, just like Grey had suggested. Which meant . . . no, he wouldn't think about going back. He and Màiri had talked about it, but right now, Ian couldn't fathom the possibility. Maybe someday.

Little by little, each of them recovered enough to sit and then stood. Grey was the first to start searching the study. "We need a phone."

"Wish I'd thought to leave mine charging before we left," Reik said, proving his dry wit hadn't suffered any damage. "Seriously, not one phone anywhere?"

Ian kissed Màiri, trying to look at the study through her eyes. He glanced over at Marian, Maggie, and Deirdre. They had pretty much the same expressions on their faces as they looked around the room at his dad's computer, even the stapler on his desk. For the millionth time, Ian tried to imagine getting pulled through time without realizing what was happening. What a nightmare.

"Mom," he said.

"Yeah, I know," Rhys said, having apparently given up his search for a charged phone. "I plugged mine in. Nothing yet."

"At least we know we didn't arrive before we left," he said, pointing to the notes Rhys had scrawled before disappearing. "We just need to figure out how much time has passed."

"And if Mom is back. If Dad is okay. And pretty much everything. Jesus," Ian said, moving toward Rhys. "How long does it take to charge a phone?"

Reik glanced back at Deirdre. "We'll need to get them some clothes."

"Them," Grey said. "How about us?"

Ian could have worn his jeans back, but he'd wanted a physical reminder of his time in the past. Plus, he'd given his old clothes to Colban, just for fun. "My clothes will fit all of us. When the phone comes on, call Jeremy first."

"Yeah, already thought of that," Reik said as Ian extended his hand to Màiri. Pulling her up, he put his arm around her waist. "Can you walk?"

She nodded. "Aye, I believe so."

Ian caught Grey's eyes. Their speech. They'd broken down everything before coming through, cooking up various stories about their absence, depending on the amount of time they'd been gone. They'd also have to explain the fact that all four of them were now married to women who sounded not just foreign, but extremely . . . well, medieval. But they had a plan for that too.

Heading off to Scotland while their dad was in the hospital wouldn't look good to the public. But Ian had come up with a story, one that offered as many truths as possible but left a good chunk to the imagination. They'd gone on an extended "emergency family trip" overseas to find a cure for their father, and they'd met their wives while abroad.

He'd call a press conference, his last for McCaim Shipping. Then, with his brothers' blessing, he and Màiri would start their nonprofit.

But their new venture was for another day. Right now they needed to find Mom and haul ass to the hospital.

"My room is this way." Ian led Màiri through the hall, its white walls a contrast to the gleaming hardwood beneath their feet. He hurried up the grand staircase that led to the second floor of the mansion where he grew up, and still lived, with his father.

Who clearly had not been back. Everything was just as they'd left it. Which was good in one way—they clearly hadn't been gone long—but part of him had hoped their parents might be here.

But they clearly hadn't been back.

"'Tis so beautiful. And bright."

Even more so on the second floor, with a large picture window greeting them at the top of the staircase. Màiri moved toward it, her eyes widening as she looked out to their courtyard and garden. From this vantage point, they could even see buildings on the other side of the gate that enclosed their property.

"Garden Street is that way. You can see the tops of buildings this way.

"'Tis like a village, of sorts. I can't wait to explore it with you. We can look for a place to house . . . whatever we decide we want to open."

"I think . . . I think I have an idea about that."

"You do?" They'd discussed it at length, and he had a few ideas, but Ian really wanted Màiri's input.

"Aye, I do. You talked about women, how they've come so far since my time, but still are not equal. And some find themselves in difficult situations. Maybe a place . . ." She shrugged, unsure of the words to use.

But he knew them exactly. "A women's shelter. We'll open a women's shelter."

He loved it. And her. "I'll tell you more about them later." He pointed up ahead. "My room is this way."

Former room soon, as they'd be looking for their own place soon.

He led her to the last room on the left and opened the door. His mother had decorated the entire house, including this room. With a four-poster bed at its center and a large white marble fireplace, his room looked just about the same as it had when his mother left.

No, not left, disappeared. Was pulled back through time.

Was she here? Ian prayed so, but he was trying to mentally prepare himself for the worst.

"Go ahead and explore. I'm gonna grab some clothes."

Walking into the closet, Ian unwrapped the plaid he still wore and undressed. He'd miss a lot of things about the past, but linen shirts weren't one of them. Pulling on jeans and a T-shirt, Ian grabbed as much as he could carry. Sweats too in case jeans didn't fit. They were all relatively the same size, but still.

"Màiri," he called, needing some help carrying the shoes. "Can you—"

She was already there, behind him.

"Your home is beautiful," she said, her color finally coming back to normal.

"You are beautiful," he countered, praying she would never regret her decision to come with him. Having her here, in his room, was unlike any feeling in the world. He'd seen the look in her eye as she said goodbye to her father—he knew how much she'd given up to be here, but he vowed to make her as comfortable and happy as possible here in his time. "I . . ."

"Come, we can talk later. I am well."

The look in her eyes, sad but understanding, told him she'd read his mind. Again. She knew he thought of her father. But she also knew he was desperate to find out about his own parents.

Without another word, they stepped back into the hall—which was when something occurred to Ian.

"If she came back . . ." He started running before he finished the thought. Just as he got past the staircase, toward his parents' bedroom, shouts from the bottom of the stairs reached him.

He didn't have to go to his parents' room to look for clues. To see if maybe she or Dad had left anything there.

Before his mind even registered Grey's words, Ian recognized the tone in which they'd been spoken. He dropped the clothes and then fell to his knees. His wife's arms wrapped around him from above as Ian began to cry like he'd never done in his whole life.

Not when Mom disappeared.

Not when Dad went into the hospital.

Not even when he was reunited with his brothers.

His mother had come up the stairs, was on the floor with him. Ian wrapped his arms around her, tears soaking her shirt.

He was so overcome, he couldn't talk. Couldn't even make a sound.

"It's okay, Ian. I'm here. Dad is awake."

Over and over his mother said the words, his brother's screams of joy at the bottom of the stairs joined now by the other McCaim brothers.

Ian didn't care that he was a blubbering fool. When he was finally able to control himself for a second, he pulled away to look at his mother. And then he pulled Màiri into their embrace, apologizing for his inability to speak.

"You've nothing to apologize for, Ian." Màiri finally stood, pulling them both up with her. His mother was here, alive. Dad was awake.

"Mom, this is my wife."

How the hell had he gotten so damn lucky?

EPILOGUE

THEY COULD BARELY fit in the room.

They'd been shoved out once by a well-meaning but no-nonsense nurse. After that, they'd tended to visit a few at a time, if only to give the staff a break. But they'd all shown up this time, and no one was budging. The nurse threw up her hands. "Fine, you can stay. But I need to listen to your dad's heart."

Nine of them went silent.

Colin McCaim had been cleared to go home today, and he was packed and ready. Then, out of nowhere, his dad had been told to sit back down. The nurse needed to check a few things first. Rhys had argued they'd already signed the paperwork. That the doctor had discharged him.

Tomorrow was Thanksgiving. And every damn one of them had more to be thankful for than ever.

Please don't let something be wrong.

Ian caught Màiri's eyes. She looked as worried as he felt. Her immediate bond with his father hadn't come as a surprise to Ian. In the two weeks they'd been back, time nearly standing still since they'd been gone, Màiri had spent as much time with his father as he had. He knew she missed her father like crazy, and it was a balm to the soul to be with her father-in-law.

His mother took his hand and squeezed it. "It's just standard procedure."

He looked at her. After two weeks, she still didn't seem real.

Shona MacKinnish. Shona McCaim. Ellen MacKinnish. So many identities, but only one of them mattered to Ian.

"Mom," he whispered, "I love you."

He'd never take those words for granted again. Nor would he take for granted the sight of the two most important women in his life standing side by side. Màiri had already come to love this city as he did. She was doing much better acclimating than he had to her time. Ian could crawl under his father's hospital bed in shame thinking about the day he'd told his wife she was free to go. The salted meat must have gotten to him. His stomach still roiled at the thought of the things they'd eaten.

As the nurse worked, he looked at his brothers.

They worried about more than spoiled meat. Each of them had endured things that would take a lifetime to fully heal. But they were on their way. Thankfully, they had someone who'd been through their hell, and worse: their mother.

"I forgot to ask," he whispered to his mother again. "Did you get in touch with that professor?"

"He got back to me this morning. I'll tell you about it later."

Ian tried to study his mother's face, but she wasn't giving much away. If her contact at the University of Edinburgh had information on Clan MacKinnish that couldn't be found in the history books at home or on the internet, Ian would have to wait to find out about it later.

So far it seemed like their escapades in the past turned out okay. No altered history, except for a few bad guys dying earlier than they would have. Màiri indeed had a brother who played a key role in the war. The thought of her father and Alana being new parents together had taken the sting out of her leaving.

Honestly, it was hard to glean as much as they'd hoped given the relative lack of documentation from that era. They'd probably never be finished digging for information, however obscure. Each of them felt connected to the past in a way they'd never thought possible. Only his father hadn't been back to medieval Scotland. Ironic since he was the one to devote five years of his life to that particular cause.

"He's all set."

The nurse looked around the room.

"We don't usually get so many family members for a discharge." She smiled at their father, who, other than being a few pounds lighter, looked no worse for wear. Thanks to Mom. Two days of listening to her stories about the past, and their sons' escapades there, had woken their dad up. He said he couldn't remember Mom talking to him. Or anything other than a few hallucinations that sounded crazier than the *your mom is a time traveler* variety. Once he was finally lucid enough to understand what was happening, Dad had to be restrained from getting out of the bed. He'd wanted to take his wife in his arms for the first time in five years.

Three weeks later, he looked ready to helm McCaim Shipping again. But he wouldn't be doing so. Happy to be retired and let his three sons run the business, Dad had said his and Mom's first order of business would be a vacation. He and Mom on a beach somewhere. They both deserved it.

"That's too bad," Reik said. "Nothing more important than family."

Ian was still getting used to the new Reik.

How long has it been since I thanked Deirdre? Probably time to do it again.

Ian smiled at Reik's wife and then leaned toward Màiri as Mom made her way to Dad's bedside. He had, of course, tried to ditch the wheelchair, but the nurse was having none of it.

"What did you guys think of the space?" he asked. In the

excitement of Dad being released this afternoon, he'd completely forgotten about Màiri's appointment. She, Marian, Maggie, and Deidre had visited yet another building, the fifth in the past week.

"We liked it. Might be the one."

"Get out!"

"I don't suppose you mean that . . . how do you say it?"

"Literally?"

"Aye. I mean yes. Literally."

"Ian." The sound of his father's gruff voice tore the smile off his face. "Wheel me out of here, will you?"

Shit.

They hadn't talked alone yet. Despite having been thrust back to a more dangerous time than Bourbon Street at 3:00 a.m. during Mardi Gras, his dad's words made Ian's heart skip a beat.

"Of course," he responded, kissing Màiri before moving toward his father. "We'll meet you guys outside."

"Downstairs," his father amended. "We'll just be a few minutes."

Ian gripped the handles of his dad's wheelchair and watched as his family, much bigger than it had been just a few weeks ago, filed out of the room one or two at a time. Well, a few weeks ago here in the present. Rhys had been in the past for just over a year, which made his brother another year older than him, a thought that still freaked him out a bit.

"Come over here."

Ian let go of the grips and sat on the bed next to his father.

"You should have told me," his dad said.

Sighing, unsure of what to say, he frowned. "You had Mom. And then all of the time travel stuff."

For which he and his brothers couldn't stop apologizing, although their father was always quick to remind them the only thing that mattered was that they were all here, together, and alive.

"You still could have told me. Apparently your brothers saw it, but I didn't. I'm sorry."

Ian shook his head. "No way. You're not allowed to be sorry. You had enough to deal with without worrying about your son not digging his job. That was nothing."

"Ian." His father reached out and took his hand. "Your happiness is everything. You, your brothers. Nothing else matters. I hope you understand that now?"

God, did he ever.

"I do."

"And we should have told you sooner about your mom."

Not this again. "Seriously, Dad. No. You guys made the best decisions you could, every step of the way. And honestly, now that I've done it, time travel isn't something I'll be talking about to anyone. Not even my own kids. It's too hard to wrap your brain around. The last thing I want is anyone to be tempted to find that cross and go skipping across time on a dangerously warped vacation. You did the right thing."

He and Màiri had talked it through many times over the past couple of weeks, sometimes alone and sometimes with the others, and they'd agreed to never go back. Not even to see the family they'd left behind. It was too risky. They had both crosses here, in the present, so there would be no visits from any travelers either.

"Your own kids?" His dad smiled. "Do you know something I don't?"

"Not yet. I'll leave that to Grey for now. We'll be busy with the foundation. And Màiri thinks we may have found a building."

"Good. We'll go look at it next week. First, a Thanksgiving meal with extra stuffing."

That had been Dad's one request for tomorrow's meal.

He had to ask.

"You're not angry?"

His dad's brows furrowed. "Angry? That my son and his wife are opening a women's shelter? Seriously, Ian? How could you ask that?"

Ian could breathe again for the first time since this whole ordeal started. All was truly well.

"Besides, when your mom and I get back from the beach, we'll need something to keep us busy. I mean it when I say the business is theirs."

Smiling, he stood, leaning down to embrace his father. They stayed that way until a knock on the door interrupted them.

So much for meeting them downstairs.

Rhys, Grey, and Reik walked inside, Reik closing the door behind him.

"We figured you were talking about Ian's foundation," Rhys said.

"And we wanted to make sure." Grey shifted his weight from one foot to the other.

"Go on," his father boomed. Even sitting in a hospital bed, he was scary as hell.

"Just . . ." Reik cleared his throat. For three tough Highlander men, his brothers had clammed up pretty quickly.

"You wanted to make sure I gave Ian my blessing?"

His father hadn't built a multibillion-dollar company by being an idiot. All four of them, Ian included, smiled.

"Aye," Rhys said, the entire room bursting into laughter. They'd traveled through time and were better men for it. And one of the two people who had given them the skills they needed to survive was joined by the other when their mom came back into the room.

"Are we having Thanksgiving dinner here in the hospital, then?"

No one spoke. Because they all thought the same thing. In this hospital room, at home . . . it didn't really matter where they ate. They were all here. Alive. Healthy.

The McCaim family, together for all time.

→ NOT READY TO LEAVE MEDIEVAL ENGLAND AND SCOTLAND YET? Click here to download The Blacksmith, the first book in Cecelia's Order of the Broken Blade series.

→ LOVE CHATTING with other romance readers? Join Cecelia's reader group, Blood & Brawn.

→ LAST BUT NOT LEAST, become a CM Insider to get a free novella + bonus content.

PREVIEW OF THE BLACKSMITH

Northumbria, England, 1214

"This is treason."

Lance said it first and wasn't surprised when no one responded. They all knew it, and speaking the word aloud again would serve no purpose.

"Think carefully before you respond." Conrad moved to the flap of the tent, peered outside, and apparently satisfied, sat back down.

So *this* was why his friend had set up so far away from the rest of the tents. Conrad had known that his proposal would turn the four of them into traitors.

"I'll do it," he said.

The earl would only have proposed such a drastic action after careful consideration, and he trusted his friend implicitly.

All three of the men watched him, none more carefully than Conrad. But he had said his piece. He wouldn't change his mind.

"We will need support." Terric had more reason to march against the king than any of them, but he was also the most cautious. He would have the most questions, but Lance was confident he would do it. They all would.

"If the Northern lords don't join together now," Conrad said, "then they are lost."

"We'll be lost too, lest you forget." Guy crossed his arms and sat back in the chair that had been carted here on a wagon filled with the luxuries afforded them by Conrad's station.

Their friend cared little for such comforts, which was why it had surprised Lance when he'd insisted on attending the Tournament of the North in such a stately fashion, something his father would have done were he still alive. Conrad was reminding those who might join their cause that the Earl of Licheford was one of the most powerful Northern border lords.

"I am no great lord," Guy continued, "but I'm as affected by John's policies as any."

"And taxes," Conrad added. "His policies and taxes. Both will be our demise if we allow it."

Guy shrugged as if their friend had asked if he wished for a meal rather than suggested they join forces against their king. "I'd not turn away an adventure such as this."

"An adventure?" Terric shook his head. "You're mad to call it one." Then, turning back to Conrad, "You have a plan?"

"The beginnings of one, aye. The most crucial part being your support."

By "your" he meant the three of them. With just one more assent, the course of each of their lives would change forever.

Terric stood and extended his arm, fist clenched. His friend had extended his arm for such a vow only once before.

Conrad clasped his wrist.

Guy was next.

Lance, last.

"Today we pledge more than a vow of silence. We form an order this day." Conrad looked directly at Terric. "The Order of the Broken Blade."

A perfect name. A symbol of the abuse of power that can

accompany a man who believes his rule divine. Nothing but silence followed his proclamation.

It was more than a name. It was a *promise*. Like the first one they made to one another many, many years ago. No one else would understand the significance, yet each of them did—and each took it to heart.

"For England," Terric said. Ironic for him to be the one to say so, as he was the only one among them not English.

Lance hated to dissent but thought it important to mention a fact Conrad seemed to have overlooked.

"An order? Of knights?"

Unclasping hands, they waited for him to finish.

"Surely you see the problem? Aye, you're an earl, and Terric's a baron's son." He nodded to Guy. "Even the mercenary is a knight."

"And my title is well earned," Guy winked, "unlike these two."

Lance couldn't help but smile at that. Guy had made the remark many times over the years. That it failed to rile Conrad now was a mark of the seriousness of their discussion.

"Take out your sword," Conrad ordered, his gaze on Lance.

There were few men Lance took orders from these days, but this man was one of them. So he complied.

He'd intended to remind Conrad he was but a blacksmith, but there was no use telling his friends what they already knew. And though Lance had no use for a fancy title or any of its trappings, the solemnity of the moment was not lost on him. No, it was clear to them all. One look at Terric's and Guy's expressions told him as much.

Ignoring the others, he dropped to one knee, laying his sword across it as Conrad pulled out his own sword. Tapping him on each shoulder, he uttered the words Lance had never thought to hear in his lifetime. When he was finished, Conrad bade him rise.

"Stand up as a knight, in the name of God."

He did, unsure what to say.

"Do you have any further opposition to our order?" Conrad asked.

"No."

"Good. We've much to discuss."

Of that, Lance had no doubt. Rebelling against a king required planning, after all.

"Including your new title." Guy bowed to him. "Sir Lance."

"I quite like it." Terric bowed as well.

"A Scots clan chief bowing to an English blacksmith." Guy looked at Conrad, raising his eyebrows dramatically. "I'll admit 'tis a sight I'll not soon forget."

"When you finish jesting . . ."

"Does he ever?" Lance asked Conrad sincerely.

"We've the small matter of King John to discuss."

Small matter indeed. If even a hint of what they'd just done were whispered to the wrong person, their heads would be forfeit for it.

Knight or blacksmith, earl or mercenary . . . none of their titles, or lack thereof, would matter if they were exposed as traitors to the crown.

———

THE KING'S men marched through the courtyard as if it were their own. Idalia's father stood next to her on the doorstep of the great keep's entrance. She peeked up at him, wondering when the hair of his beard had become more gray than black.

"Welcome," he boomed as the first of the newcomers reached

them. A captain, perhaps? Idalia tried not to smile at the looks they were receiving. Not outright hostility, but certainly the people of Stanton could give the representatives of the king a warmer welcome.

She was secretly glad they did not.

"My lord." The tall, thin captain bowed to her father, the Earl of Stanton. "We travel to Norham Castle and request shelter for the evening."

Interesting. Why were the king's men on their way to Norham and so far north?

Idalia could hear her father's silent answer to her silent question. *Do not concern yourself with the affairs of men.* She also knew what he would say next.

"My daughter will see to your comfort." He looked at her as if expecting a retort. It was market day, her favorite, and Father knew it well.

But he knew his daughter too.

"Of course." She smiled as the captain and his two companions joined her. They were dressed identically, in armor topped with bright red tunics bearing the crest of their king. They'd require assistance in removing that armor. Marina, her mother's maid, would normally assist her in making the arrangements, but Marina was nowhere to be seen.

More likely than not, she was sitting at Idalia's mother's bedside, something the maid often chided her for doing.

I have been her maid for as many years as you are alive, she would say. Which was not fully correct—Idalia had only been alive for two and twenty years, and Marina had been her mother's most trusted servant for four years longer. Sometimes it felt as if Idalia had two mothers.

"Follow me," she instructed the men, catching her father's small smile. Seeing one of his rare smiles almost made missing market day worthwhile.

Taking them past the great stairs on either side of the

entranceway to the keep, Idalia nearly missed the flash of royal blue.

Her younger sister. She wished to call out to Tilly, but it was unlikely she'd get a response. Tilly disliked helping with the duties about Stanton. Sure enough, the flash of blue was there and then gone.

By the time she showed the men to their chambers and sent up a squire to assist them with their armor, Dawson, the seneschal, had already spoken to Cook about dinner and arranged baths for the three men.

His help had eased the burden of the unexpected guests, but Idalia had one more thing to do before she could check on her mother. The captain had made a special request of her—or rather, of the smith. She left the great keep and walked through the courtyard down to the castle forge. Stepping around puddles that had formed on the gravel path after that morning's rain, she arrived, the door, as always, already open.

"Daryon," she said, stepping into the darkened room. "Is there enough light to repair a shoe?"

The apprentice looked up, hammer in hand. His brother had already begun tidying up. It was a habit Roland had instilled in his apprentices. Idalia pushed the thought away. When she thought of how the blacksmith had suffered before he'd succumbed to an illness all had known would claim him someday, a familiar pang in her chest reminded her of the master smith's absence.

"Aye, my lady." He looked at her hand.

"I don't have it with me but will send it straightaway. 'Tis for the king's captain," she added.

"Shall I fetch it from the stables?" the lad's twin brother, Miles, asked. At only ten and two, the boys were carrying a responsibility that should never have been asked of them. Two apprentices smithing for a castle the size of Stanton . . . she shook her head. The situation could have been avoided had her father taken Roland's illness more seriously. They should have started looking for a new master smith long ago.

"Aye, thank you. The new master should be arriving any day now." A replacement smith had finally been found at this year's Tournament of the North, a yearly event where English knights and Scottish warriors prepared for the very real battles they would later fight.

She wanted the boys to know their hard work had not gone unnoticed. "My father is grateful for your service in the interim."

As expected, both boys beamed at the praise. And it was true. Although her father rarely seemed to notice her own service to Stanton, he did recognize the boys were much too young for their current position. They were only in their third year of seven in training.

Daryon watched his brother leave. Unlike most others in the keep, Idalia could easily tell the two boys apart, and it was that look that made it so easy. Daryon was by far the more serious of the two.

The boy's thoughtful eyes darted from the doorway to her. "'Tis market day."

And Idalia never missed one if she had the choice.

"Aye, but we must see to our royal visitors," she said.

Three years earlier, her father had received a charter for Stanton to be designated a market town, courtesy of the well-maintained old Roman roads that led both north and south as well as east and west. Many castles did not enjoy such a right, especially in the "wilds" of Northern England, and Idalia was grateful for their good fortune. She visited the market as one of her duties for Stanton—her mother was much too ill to do so. Secretly, she also hoped she would one day find the herb or tonic that might help her mother. The market attracted all sorts, after all. To make such inquiries directly was impossible, however, as her father had forbidden her from speaking of her mother's worsening condition to anyone.

"Had I known, I would have gone yesterday," she said. The market day was actually poorly named—it had grown in popularity enough to stretch to two days. "And if the new master does not have the drift you need, I promise to secure your tool on the next market day."

"Thank you, my lady."

She could tell Daryon was anxious to get back to work, so she left him to it, intent on visiting with her mother before supper.

And that was when she saw him, the most handsome man she'd ever seen, striding downhill toward the forge.

Toward her.

Click here to download *The Blacksmith* to continue reading!

ALSO BY CECELIA MECCA

ORDER OF THE BROKEN BLADE

The Blacksmith

The Mercenary

The Scot

The Earl

The Chief

BORDER SERIES

The Ward's Bride

The Thief's Countess

The Lord's Captive

The Chief's Maiden

The Scot's Secret

The Earl's Entanglement

The Warrior's Queen

The Protector's Promise

The Rogue's Redemption

The Guardian's Favor

The Knight's Reward

Box Set 1 (Books 1-3)

Box Set 2 (Books 4-6)

Box Set 3 (Books 7-10)

TIME TRAVEL & PARANORMAL

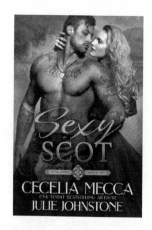

Highlander's Through Time

Sexy Scot

Scandalous Scot

Enchanted Falls

Falling for the Knight

Bloodwite (Contemporary PNR)

The Vampire's Temptation

The Immortal's Salvation

The Hunter's Affection

ABOUT THE AUTHOR

Cecelia Mecca is the author of medieval romance, including the Border Series, and sometimes wishes she could be transported back in time to the days of knights and castles. Although the former English teacher's actual home is in Northeast Pennsylvania where she lives with her husband and two children, her online home can be found at CeceliaMecca.com. She would love to hear from you.

 facebook.com/ceceliamecca
twitter.com/ceceliamecca
instagram.com/ceceliamecca